PRAISE FOR GEOFFREY M COOPER

Advance Praise for *The Plagiarism Plot*

"Another spectacular medical thriller by Geoffrey M Cooper, *The Plagiarism Plot* will have readers eyeballs deep in this multifaceted mystery. Fast-paced and well detailed, this is a book that readers won't want to put down." —Kristi Elizabeth, *Manhattan Book Review*

"*The Plagiarism Plot* takes clinical research and scientific motives to a whole new level with its intricate story and likable main characters." —Kathryn Dare, *San Francisco Book Review*

"Cooper's eighth installment in the Brad Parker and Karen Richmond series is a riveting tale of ambition, betrayal, and ethical quandaries set against the backdrop of academic research. Cooper blends technical precision with narrative tension, offering a gripping portrayal of the academic world with its pressures, ambitions, and moral lapses." —*The Prairies Book Review*

Praise for Earlier Books in the Brad Parker and Karen Richmond Series

Nondisclosure
"One of this year's best mysteries by a Maine writer . . . a gritty mystery, well-crafted with a complex, intriguing plot, tense suspense, vivid action and wholly believable characters." —Bill Bushnell, *Central Maine Sentinel*

Forever
"A medical thriller on the lines of a Robin Cook–style saga . . . designed to keep readers on edge to its satisfying conclusion." —D. Donovan, *Midwest Book Review*

"A persuasive tale of scientific intrigue." —*Kirkus Reviews*

Bad Medicine
"Plot twists and fast-paced action make this a fun yet scary story."
—Bill Bushnell, *Central Maine Sentinel*
"A noteworthy whodunit with unexpected plot twists." —*Kirkus Reviews*

Ill Intent
"A whodunit that effortlessly navigates a complex plot and deepens its narrator's characterization." —*Kirkus Reviews*
"A medical thriller that is firmly rooted in psychological interactions and unexpected developments." —D. Donovan, *Midwest Book Review*

Perilous Obsession
"*Perilous Obsession* is Ogunquit author Geoffrey Cooper's fifth mystery in his thriller series featuring Brad Parker and FBI Special Agent Karen Richmond. And this is probably the best one of all." —Bill Bushnell, *Central Maine Sentinel*
"An often-exciting tale of medical malfeasance and wide-ranging criminality." —*Kirkus Reviews*

The Fifth Student
"College students cheating on a test sizzles into something far more complex and deadly in the latest thriller from Geoffrey Cooper." —Matt Cost, award-winning author of *Velma Gone Awry* and the Clay Wolfe/Port Essex and Mainely Mystery series.
"A zippy, tricky academic murder mystery." —*Kirkus Reviews*

The Third Man
"Falling between Robin Cook's medical thrillers and Robert Parker's Spenser potboilers isn't a bad place to live—and this one hits a sweet spot." —*Blue Ink Review*
"There are many mirrors between this book's thriller and suspense

action and real-world headlines today. Perhaps that's what makes it especially intriguing and frightening and hard to put down." —D. Donovan, *Midwest Book Review*

ALSO BY GEOFFREY M COOPER

The Prize

Nondisclosure

Forever

Bad Medicine

Ill Intent

Perilous Obsession

The Fifth Student

The Third Man

THE PLAGIARISM PLOT

A MEDICAL THRILLER

BRAD PARKER AND KAREN RICHMOND
BOOK 8

GEOFFREY M COOPER

CAPTAIN THOMAS PUBLISHING

ISBN 978-1-7337714-4-3 (paperback)

ISBN 978-1-7337714-5-0 (e-book)

THE PLAGIARISM PLOT

PROLOGUE

A woman wearing a TSA badge approached as she got off the plane in Washington. After verifying her identity, the woman led the way to a conference room on the terminal's lower level. Monica followed, her stomach doing flip-flops with anxiety about the meeting she was here to attend.

She remembered when it had all started several weeks ago. The man she called Mr. Black had been waiting outside the Biological Sciences Building when she left work. It had been a bad day, and she was feeling even more frustrated than usual with the unsatisfactory progress of her research. Especially because her evaluation for tenure was about to begin, and she harbored no illusions as to how it would turn out. She'd published some solid papers, but they were all in mid-level journals and none of them represented a significant breakthrough. Given her failure to produce a single major publication in a high-impact journal, it was virtually certain that she'd be denied tenure, and her employment at Westmark University would be terminated. After that, it was highly unlikely that she'd be able to find another job in research. Maybe she could become a high school biology teacher. Or an Uber driver.

The man was tall and thin, distinctively dressed in a black silk suit worn over a black polo shirt. They'd never met before, but he seemed to know all about her situation and had offered to help. With nothing to lose, she agreed to accompany him to a nearby park where they could talk privately. What he wanted from her was complicated but doable. And he offered a reward that was irresistible. If she did as he asked, his boss would get her a tenured position at a major research university. The kind of position she didn't seem able to get on her own.

It sounded too good to be true, which she figured meant it was probably bullshit. But she couldn't bring herself to just walk away, so she'd probed further.

"I don't even know who you are. Why should I believe you can get me a job?" she'd challenged him.

"Not a bad question. You don't need to know my name. And it's better for you if you don't know who I'm working for. But I can offer you a token of good faith. One that will demonstrate our sincerity."

"What, an envelope of hundred-dollar bills?" she'd scoffed. "That's a lot different than a tenured professorship."

"No. Something that will demonstrate our influence in academic circles. And our ability to deliver what we promise."

She'd raised an eyebrow, and he continued. "I understand you have a paper being considered for publication in *Cancer Treatment*. Unfortunately, it received negative reviews from the outside experts who evaluated your manuscript and was rejected. You wrote to the editor trying to rebut their criticisms, but we both know that's unlikely to succeed, and you'll be receiving a final rejection letter soon."

He was sadly correct. Submitting to *Cancer Treatment*, the leading journal in her field, had been a long shot, but she'd given it a try because getting published there would probably be all she needed to put her over the tenure bar. But she'd known the paper wasn't good enough, and the reviewers had unequivocally agreed.

She'd shrugged, trying to put on a brave front. "We'll see. You can never tell what an editor will do. Maybe he'll at least get some new reviews."

"If you agree to work with us, I can tell you *exactly* what the editor will do. He'll accept your paper for immediate publication."

She'd felt her jaw drop. "You can do that?"

"Of course. If you join us, you'll have that letter of acceptance within a few days. After that, you'll receive the invitation to serve on the National Institutes of Health grant review panel that we discussed. And not too long from now, when you're finished with your part in this, your new position will be waiting."

If the man had the kind of power needed to influence the editor of *Cancer Treatment*, his offer was too good to pass up. Just the acceptance of her paper would probably be enough to get her tenure at Westmark. Even if it didn't, a publication in *Cancer Treatment* would make it easy for her to get a tenured job at another institution.

What they wanted from her was straightforward enough, although he hadn't told her *why* they wanted her to do it. When she'd asked, he insisted that she didn't need to know, which hadn't left her feeling good about it. Still, her part in whatever they were planning wasn't all that bad in the big picture of scientific misconduct. At least the part that NIH would know about. She'd undoubtedly receive some kind of reprimand, but that was nothing compared to the reward he offered.

She'd taken a deep breath and agreed to do as he asked.

"A wise decision." He'd handed her a cell phone. "We'll use this phone to communicate. I've put my number and email address in the contacts. If you need to speak to me, just leave a message asking for Mr. Jones, and I'll get back to you. I've also set up an untraceable email account that you can use to send me a copy of the grant."

Her sense of humor had started to return, and she'd smiled. "No, Mr. Jones is too ordinary a name for you. I'll call you Mr. Black, after your suit and shirt."

Her paper had been promptly accepted, the invitation from NIH had arrived, and she'd followed Mr. Black's instructions. Not long after the paper came out, her department chair had called her into his office to tell her how impressed he was by seeing her work published in the leading journal in her field. That was exactly what she needed for her tenure case, which he assured her was now quite strong and had just received a positive vote from the department faculty. It still had to go through university-level review, but he didn't anticipate any problems.

That had been just over a week ago, and she'd been giddy with the realization that the tenured position she'd coveted was finally hers. But now it was payback time, and she steeled herself for her final part in whatever scheme Mr. Black had put in motion.

When they reached their destination, her TSA escort let her into a room where two men and a woman were seated at a small metal conference table. She recognized the woman as Dr. Johansen, the NIH administrator who ran the grant review committee on which she'd served. She didn't know either of the men, both of whom wore dark suits and ties and regarded her with cold, unsmiling faces.

Dr. Johansen gestured to a seat at the end of the table, offered her a bottle of water, and took the lead. "Thank you for joining us, Monica. As you know, this meeting concerns your service on the Clinical Therapeutics grant review panel. Drs. Thorsten and Weinstein here are investigators from the ORI. You know what that is?"

"The Office of Research Integrity. But why is ORI interested in my work on your study section?"

Thorsten cleared his throat. "If you don't mind, we'd prefer to ask the questions. More efficient that way. When you were on that study section, did you review a grant submitted by Garrett Jackson?"

"I did," she replied. "The application dealt with using computational methods to identify drugs for cancer chemotherapy. I remember it was quite a good grant."

Thorsten eyed her coldly. "We're aware. And we're also aware that you emailed a copy to Carolyn Gelman at MTRI. The Maine Translational Research Institute."

Mr. Black had warned her they'd know that she'd emailed the grant to Carolyn but told her to look surprised. When she did, the other ORI investigator broke in before she could answer. "Don't bother trying to deny it. We've already obtained a copy of your email from your university's server."

Now Monica pretended to be flustered. "I'm sorry. Carolyn's in my field, and we've become friends. There was a section of the application that was similar to some of the things she's working on, so I sent it to her to see what she thought of it."

Johansen broke in with a heavy sigh. "Oh, Monica, I made it very clear when you joined the study section that the NIH rules of confidentiality explicitly prohibit reviewers from sharing applications with anyone other than panel members. How could you ignore that?"

"I just wanted to get her input so I could evaluate the grant fairly. I didn't mean any harm. Anyway, she emailed back that it would be inappropriate for her to read the application. She said she was just going to delete it."

Thorsten pushed two pieces of paper across the table toward her. "Are these the emails?"

The first was from Monica to Carolyn Gelman and had Jackson's grant application attached.

Hi Carolyn, I hope all is well. I'm on an NIH review panel and would be grateful for your help in evaluating one of my grants, which I've attached. In particular, the experiments in section two are just the kind of thing you do. Could you take a look and let me know what you think? Thanks so much, Monica

The reply was terse and to the point.

As you should know, it's against NIH rules for you to send me a grant you're reviewing. I'm going to just delete it. I won't tell anyone, but please don't do anything like this again.

"And that's all you heard from Gelman?" Thorsten asked.

Monica nodded. "That was it."

Weinstein followed up with the next question. "Did you send the grant to anyone else?"

This was where Mr. Black had told her she'd have to lie. They couldn't know about the copy she'd sent him from the secure account on the phone. "No. When Carolyn couldn't help me, I just reviewed the grant as best I could on my own. I didn't mean to do anything wrong."

Weinstein exchanged glances with Thorsten, who nodded in response to some unspoken question. Then he continued. "All right, Monica. We understand that you intended no harm, but the fact remains that you broke one of the principal rules governing the conduct of NIH reviewers. We're going to have to issue a formal warning, which will be kept on file in case there are any problems in the future. Do you have any questions?"

When she said no, they thanked her for her cooperation and told her she could go. Once she was alone, walking back to the gate for her return flight to Boston, she used the phone Mr. Black had given her to call and leave a message saying that everything had gone just as he'd predicted. Then she tossed the phone into a nearby waste can. Now that she had tenure, she had no need for further support from Mr. Black or his boss.

She knew she should be feeling good, but she couldn't shake a sense of unease. Not when she didn't know what they were plotting.

CHAPTER 1

pulled into the MTRI parking lot a few minutes before nine. Late for me, but I'd lingered on the beach, enjoying a long walk with my pug, Rosie. Early September was my favorite time of year in Maine. Labor Day signaled the end of the summer tourist crowd, and US 1 in Wells was back to normal instead of looking like a crowded parking lot. We could once again get into our favorite restaurants, even on weekends. The summer heat and humidity had been replaced with cool nights and pleasant days. And, perhaps most important to me, we were in the midst of fall bird migration. Shorebirds stopping off on their journey south were abundant, and rich displays of sandpipers, herons, and egrets had kept Rosie and me at the beach this morning.

I went to the director's suite on the first floor to start the day, anticipating a relatively light schedule. Only to be surprised when my administrative assistant, Anna, told me that two visitors from the NIH Office of Research Integrity, Drs. Thorsten and Weinstein, had called late yesterday afternoon when I was out to make an appointment. They were already here, and they looked important, so she'd invited them to wait in my office.

I sighed inwardly. They probably wanted me to serve on some kind of committee to review a misconduct case. Or maybe to draft policy recommendations. Either way, I was pretty sure it would be something I'd rather not spend time on. But I couldn't very well decline a request from NIH when they provided most of the institute's funding.

Taking a deep breath, I went in to find them sitting at my conference table. They were both wearing suits and ties, which looked out of place in the informal atmosphere of MTRI.

"Good morning, I'm Brad Parker," I greeted them. We exchanged handshakes, and they introduced themselves as Stuart Thorsten and David Weinstein. Then I took my customary seat at the head of the table and asked how I could help them.

Thorsten took the lead. "We're here to inform you that an allegation of misconduct has been made against one of your faculty members. We've done an initial assessment and concluded that the accusation is credible. The next step is to ask you, as director of MTRI, to undertake an institutional investigation."

I sat up with a start. This was the last thing I'd expected. Since I'd been director, there had been a few cases of authorship disputes or graduate students being too selective about which data to include in their theses. But nothing that rose to the level of an official ORI misconduct inquiry.

I shook my head in an effort to get this into focus. "I'm sorry, you caught me by surprise. We've only had some minor problems that I've dealt with internally before. Can you tell me what's going on?"

"Of course," Weinstein said. "That's what we're here for. The case involves plagiarism. The investigator whose work was stolen discussed using computational methods to identify targeted anticancer drugs in a grant application. A related approach was used in a paper from your faculty member that was brought to our attention. We looked into the matter and after comparing the grant application with the published paper, we agreed there were clear similarities."

My reaction to that was that it didn't mean much. I shrugged in response. "I see. But I'm sure you're aware there are many instances of two scientists independently developing closely related methods or doing nearly identical experiments. It seems that sometimes a field's ripe for a new idea, and that idea comes to more than one person at a time."

Thorsten gave me an annoyed look. "We're well aware of that, and the similarities between the grant and the publication wouldn't be a credible basis for allegations of plagiarism by themselves. But we took it one step further and looked into whether your faculty member had access to the grant proposal, which should have been seen only by members of the study section that reviewed the application."

"And were they on the study section?" I asked.

"They were not. But we also asked the reviewers' home institutions to examine their emails to see if they'd sent out anything about the application."

"That seems like a long shot," I said. "If someone was going to send an email that violated grant confidentiality, they'd be smart enough to use a private account rather than their institutional email."

Thorsten smiled. "We thought so too but figured it wouldn't hurt to check. And it paid off. We found that an email with a copy of the grant was sent by one of the reviewers to your faculty member. We then questioned the reviewer, who admitted that she'd sent out the application asking for your faculty member's assistance with her review."

Now I understood. "That's awful! It's completely contrary to what researchers applying for a grant have a right to expect. And I certainly see why you need to look into the matter. Who's the MTRI faculty member in question?"

"I'll only be able to reveal that if you agree to conduct an investigation."

"If an MTRI faculty member is guilty of this kind of misconduct, I want to deal with them as much as you do," I assured him. "I'll appoint a faculty committee to work with me, and if allegations of plagiarism are substantiated, our policies would call for termination of the guilty party."

Thorsten looked relieved. "Good. Then we can go ahead and share our information with you."

"Starting with the name of your faculty member," Weinstein added. "Carolyn Gelman."

Carolyn Gelman! I struggled to contain the shock I felt. Carolyn wasn't only one of the institute's outstanding scientists but also my closest friend and most trusted advisor on the MTRI faculty. I knew her well enough to be confident that she'd never do anything like this. The ORI investigators obviously had something screwed up.

I started to say so but stopped myself. Protesting her innocence at this point wouldn't convince Thorsten and Weinstein. They'd just conclude that I was prejudiced. A better course was to go ahead and launch an investigation, which would no doubt establish Carolyn's innocence.

"I'm a bit surprised by that, but okay," I said. "I know Carolyn pretty well, and she doesn't seem the type. But credible allegations like this need to be thoroughly investigated. I assume the matter will be kept confidential until we reach a conclusion?"

Weinstein nodded vigorously. "Absolutely. She's innocent until proven guilty, and we don't want anyone's reputation damaged by premature leaks. Now, let us show you what we have."

Thorsten withdrew a manila folder from his briefcase and placed it on the table. "We'll leave this with you, but I'll walk you through it in case you have any questions. To start, here are printouts of the emails from the study section member to Gelman and her reply."

I examined the emails. The first asked for Carolyn's help in evaluating an attached grant. The second was Carolyn's unequivocal refusal, which seemed fine to me.

"Gelman's response is pretty clear," I said. "She admonishes the sender and says that she's going to delete the application. I don't see any problem with that."

"I agree, although she should have reported the incident to NIH," Weinstein responded. "But more to the point, while she says that she'll delete the application, there's no evidence that she didn't copy it first for later use."

Thorsten put two more documents in front of me. "These are copies of the grant and Gelman's paper. Incidentally, we're not sure if the applicant—Garrett Jackson—is the one who brought the case to our attention. The allegations were anonymous, although they must have come from either Jackson or a colleague who knew what was in the proposal." He opened both documents to pages that had been marked with yellow stickies. "These sections are where the alleged plagiarism occurred. I think you'll see what we mean if you compare the two."

I took a few minutes to look it over. The indicated parts of both the grant and the paper dealt with computational approaches to identifying candidate drugs, but the details were over my head.

"I'm afraid I don't understand this kind of analysis well enough to make a judgment," I admitted. "They're clearly both computational, but I can't tell whether there's an indication of plagiarism here or not."

Thorsten frowned. "I'm confused. I thought identification of anti-cancer drugs was your area of research."

"It is. But the use of computational methods is new to the field, and that's the part I don't follow," I explained. "I'm a classical experimentalist with no training in computer science or bioinformatics. I'd need to collaborate with someone if I wanted to do computational work."

"I have the same problem," Weinstein acknowledged. "It will probably take someone with appropriate computational background and training to evaluate the science. But given that the grant was pirated, there's reason for concern."

"Understood. We'll get someone with the necessary expertise to participate in our investigation. But there's another problem. I don't think Gelman knows any more about this kind of computation than I do. It's probably the work of one of her collaborators, not something she did herself."

"Then you'll need to determine if she shared the grant with whoever was responsible for this part of the paper," Thorsten said. "And if so, we'll work with you to figure out how to apportion the blame between Gelman and her collaborator."

I nodded. "Okay, I think I've got it."

"Is there anything further you need from us at this point, then?" Weinstein asked.

I assured them that I had what I needed to get started and promised to keep them informed as our investigation proceeded.

CHAPTER 2

When they were gone, I went over to look out the window while I revised my plan for the day. I'd been hoping to spend some time in my lab, but that would have to wait while I got the investigation started. Unpleasant though it would be, delaying wouldn't help. I needed to get a faculty committee set up, and then I had to tell Carolyn what was going on.

While I was rehearsing that conversation, a broad-winged hawk landed in one of the pine trees outside my office. Another migrant, stopping off on its way to South America. I'd have to find time in the next few weeks to make a trip to Mount Agamenticus, whose nearby summit was a great place to watch hawks soaring by on their way south. But that would need to wait for another day.

The first thing I had to do now was find someone to serve as chair of a faculty committee—a task for which Roz Seymour seemed like the logical choice. Roz was a highly accomplished scientist who was well respected by her colleagues both within and outside of MTRI. I was comfortable that she would be fair and objective as committee chair, and equally important, that I could work with her in that capacity.

After Anna called to verify that Roz was available, I went up to her office on the fifth floor. Not unexpectedly, her initial response was to turn me down, saying that she was far too busy to accept such a distasteful and time-consuming assignment. But after I explained the situation, she changed her mind. She didn't believe that Carolyn was guilty of stealing ideas from someone else's grant any more than I did, but she recognized that a thorough investigation was the best way to resolve the issue. We discussed other potential committee members and agreed that at least one of them had to have a strong computational background. She had a couple of people in mind, and I left her to begin rounding them up.

That left me with the hardest of my tasks, talking to Carolyn. I found myself hoping she wasn't in. Maybe I could put off meeting with her until tomorrow. But her door was ajar when I reached her office, so I took a deep breath, knocked, and went in.

She greeted me with a smile as I stopped to pet Molly, the enormous Newfoundland whose bed occupied a large fraction of the office floor. I'd rescued Molly a few years ago after her owner had been murdered. Rather than taking her to a shelter, I brought her to MTRI and introduced her to Carolyn, who was recently divorced. As I'd hoped, they immediately fell in love, and Molly had a new home. I always wondered if the excited tail-thumping greetings she gave me were to thank me for getting her and Carolyn together.

Carolyn echoed my thoughts. "She really loves you, Brad. Think it's because she knows you're the one who matched us up?"

I smiled and shrugged my shoulders. "Maybe. Who knows what dogs think, or how much they understand? Sometimes I think they know everything we do."

"I won't argue. But did you stop by to talk or just to say hi to Molly?"

Her blue eyes were twinkling with amusement, and her suntanned face made her look younger than her forty-two years. I knew the tan was from frequent weekend trips to a nearby lake with her kids. Carolyn had told me she liked the lake because the kids and Molly could play their favorite game. One of the kids would swim out and pretend to be drowning, flailing their arms and calling for help. Molly would jump up, race into the lake, and swim to them as fast as she could. When she reached the apparent victim, she'd turn around, let them grab her around the neck, and tow them safely back to shore. She was smart enough to know after a couple of times that they weren't really drowning, but she seemed more than happy to do it over and over again, apparently enjoying it as much as Carolyn's kids did.

It was fun to think of the kids playing with Molly, but like Mount Agamenticus, that was a thought for another day. I brought myself back to the moment and pulled a chair out from the wall.

"To talk," I said. "About something serious, I'm afraid."

Carolyn's smile faded. "Okay. What's up?"

Beating around the bush wouldn't help, so I jumped right in. "I had a visit from two investigators from the NIH Office of Research Integrity earlier today. Directing me to investigate plagiarism charges that have been brought against you."

Her eyes widened. "What?! That's absurd. You don't believe it, do you?"

I hastened to reassure her. "Of course not. But I know you, and ORI doesn't. The best way to clear it up is for me to do as they ask and establish your innocence."

She gripped the arms of her chair tightly, and I could tell she was struggling to stay in control. But she kept her voice steady. "All right, I can see that. What do they say I've done?"

"Let's go through it one piece at a time," I suggested. "The first thing they have is evidence that a member of a study section sent you a copy of a grant she was reviewing. Do you recall anything like that?"

"Sure, it was Monica Kushman. So stupid. She sent me the grant to ask for my help in evaluating it. Totally inappropriate and I wrote back telling her so. She's relatively junior and probably didn't know any better, but I hope it isn't something she repeats. Is she in trouble with ORI too?"

"I'm not sure; we didn't discuss her situation. I don't think it's too serious, although I imagine she'll be reprimanded. But the important thing is, they say you used information from the application in one of your recent papers."

She shook her head vehemently. "That's nonsense. I deleted the application immediately. I should still have the email I sent back to Monica if you want to see that."

"The ORI people already have it." I handed her the printout Thorsten had given me. "Is this it?"

She looked at it and nodded. "So are they saying I didn't really delete it? I can't show you on my computer, since it's long gone, but you could have IT verify that on the MTRI server."

"We will. But unfortunately, that won't rule out the possibility that you copied it first."

She turned red and sat up on the edge of her chair, looking like she was about to pounce. "For Christ's sake! How can you think I'd do something like that?!"

I held up both hands. "I don't, Carolyn. Not for a minute. I'm on your side. But I don't have any choice other than to investigate these allegations. If I don't, ORI will just constitute a committee of their own. At least this way, I can be sure the case is handled quickly and fairly."

She took a deep breath and sat back. "All right. I'm sorry, I know this isn't your fault. It's just . . . it's damned scary to be accused of something like this. What exactly are they saying I stole, anyway?"

I took out my copies of Jackson's grant and her paper and opened them to the relevant sections. "The claim is that you plagiarized Jackson's computational approach. Unfortunately, this kind of work is way over my head, so I can't tell how close your paper and his grant really are."

"It's over my head too," Carolyn said. "I don't do this kind of stuff; it was done by Ian Norwood. He's a bioinformatics guy at the University of Maine in Orono. One of the coauthors on the paper."

"I thought this might be the work of a collaborator. Would the study section member have sent him a copy of the grant too?"

"No, I can't imagine her sending it to Ian. She knows me because we've gone to a number of meetings together and become friends. But I don't think she knows Ian."

I started to see how I might be able to resolve this. "Then, just playing devil's advocate with ORI being the devil, the accusation would have to be that you sent a copy of the grant to Ian, and then he used Jackson's methods."

"Which I didn't, of course. And you can verify on the server that I never sent him anything like that."

I nodded and pursed my lips. "We'll do that. But ORI would just argue that you were smart enough to use a private account instead of MTRI email. Talking to Ian should help though. In addition to confirming that you didn't send him the grant, he can hopefully show us how his work differs from what's in it. I'll try to go see him tomorrow, along with Roz Seymour. She's going to chair the institutional investigation committee."

"She's a good choice for that," Carolyn agreed. "But does she have the right background to make sense of the science?"

"No, she's like you and me. But she's going to get at least one computational type to serve on the committee. With luck, they can go with us tomorrow too. Maybe we can get this damned thing cleared up quickly."

"I hope so. I feel awful, having something like this hanging over me. Do many people know about it?"

At least I could reassure her on that score. "No. We'll keep the whole thing completely confidential. And the ORI investigators are doing the same."

She looked relieved. "Well, I guess I should thank you, Brad. Shitty as this is, I'm glad you're handling it."

I gave her a wink as I got up. "I won't say it's a pleasure, but I want to dispense with it quickly and confidentially."

I patted Molly on my way out. That hadn't gone too badly, and the fact that the critical analysis had been done by one of her collaborators rather than by Carolyn was good news.

When I got back to my office, I put in a call to Ian Norwood. He was hesitant when I told him I needed to clarify some questions that had been raised about his paper with Carolyn, but in the end, he reluctantly agreed to meet with me tomorrow.

Then I called Roz to give her an update. She agreed that talking to Norwood was a good next step and was available to accompany me. She'd already recruited a computational scientist for the committee, a collaborator of hers from the Roux Institute in Portland, and would try to get him to join us as well.

I was more than ready to call it a day by the time I got off the phone. All I wanted now was to go home and talk the situation through with Karen, whose thoughts as a detective always helped me sort things out. Especially a situation as messy and fraught with conflict as this.

CHAPTER 3

Karen's red Volvo SUV was parked in the driveway when I reached our house on Drakes Island, and I felt the tingle of excitement I always got when I was about to see her. The two of us had been a couple for several years now, first living together in Boston and then moving to Maine when I took the job of MTRI director. Karen had been an FBI agent and had transferred from Boston to the Portland field office, then moved a couple of years ago to her current position in the state police as commanding officer of one of Maine's three major crimes units. Neither of us wanted to get married, having suffered through disastrous first marriages, but I'd surprised her with a ring two years ago, so we could now call each other fiancés as well as partners.

It was a nice evening, and the beach was one of the things we most enjoyed about living in Southern Maine, so when neither Karen nor Rosie greeted me at the front door, I figured that's where I'd find them. I stopped in the kitchen to pour myself a tumbler of Oban, my favorite single malt scotch, and then went through the living room and out the glass slider to our deck. From there, I could see Karen sitting on a large rock down by the ocean, her shoulder-length blond hair blowing gently in the breeze.

I took off my shoes, went down the half-dozen steps leading from the deck to the beach, and started walking over to her, only to be interrupted midway by Rosie racing over and jumping on me so hard that I spilled half my drink. That caught Karen's attention, and she was still laughing when I reached her.

She kissed me and wrinkled her nose. "Been hanging around drinking scotch all day, Professor? You smell like a brewery."

"You can thank Rosie for that. She apparently decided I should wear my scotch instead of drinking it." Taking a sip, I added, "At least she left me half a glass."

"You look like you could use it. Tough day?"

I sat down next to her. "Very. A bizarre problem with Carolyn."

"With Carolyn? That's odd, what's going on?"

"It's both odd and complicated. I want your advice on it, but it's a long story. Should we go in and do something about dinner first?"

She shrugged. "We're okay. It's only a little after six, and I stopped at the Thai place on the way home, so dinner's ready when we are. We've got at least another forty-five minutes until the sun goes down, so if Rosie left you enough scotch, let's talk out here." Picking up a glass next to her, she added, "I'm all set with my wine."

"Sounds good, I'll try to make my remaining scotch last. Today's mess started with a surprise visit by two investigators from the NIH Office of Research Integrity. They've received allegations of research misconduct against Carolyn and want me to launch an institutional investigation."

Karen looked as shocked as I'd felt. "Carolyn? Research misconduct? That's absurd. What's she supposed to have done?"

"I know, I was floored by it too. They're accusing her of having plagiarized material from another investigator's grant application."

"Plagiarism?" She furrowed her brow. "Like Harvard fired their president for? I didn't think scientists copied passages of text from each other."

"In science, it's usually a matter of stealing someone's ideas rather than copying their words," I explained. "In this case, Carolyn's being accused of stealing a drug discovery method from a grant that got sent to her."

"That's ridiculous! I may not know as much about her science as you do, but I'm close to her too. And after all my years of police work, I'm not a bad judge of character. There's just no way she'd do something like that."

"I agree, no question. But ORI isn't going to take our word for it. The best thing I can do is to investigate and establish her innocence as quickly as possible."

I went ahead and told her everything I knew so far. She listened attentively, finally breaking in when I got to the end of my meeting with Carolyn.

"Wait a minute. If Carolyn wasn't the one responsible for the section of the paper that's supposed to have been stolen, she's off the hook, right?"

"Unless she sent the grant to her collaborator. She firmly denies that she did, but I need to independently verify that."

Karen nodded. "Okay, that makes sense. What's your next move then?"

"I'm going to talk to the collaborator. He's at the University of Maine in Orono. He was reluctant to talk to me at first but somewhat grudgingly agreed to meet tomorrow. Roz is going to come too, and hopefully she'll get her computational guy to join us."

"It's interesting that he agreed to talk to you, since he's not in your institute, and you don't have any authority over him. Do you think that means he doesn't have anything to hide?"

"I sure as hell hope so. If the accusations are bullshit, it would make sense for him to want to do everything he can to remove the cloud hanging over their work. I'm hoping he'll be able to confirm that he never got anything from Carolyn. And probably even more important, that he can go over his work with Roz's computational expert and convince him that it was independent of what was in the grant. That would be the end of it."

"That'd be great," Karen said. But I could tell from her face that something was troubling her.

"You look like something's the matter. What're you thinking?" I asked.

"I'm not sure, but it feels more complicated. Like someone's manipulating things from behind a curtain. I can understand Carolyn's friend sending her the grant out of stupidity. And I can imagine how another scientist might have felt scooped by Carolyn's work and made a false allegation of plagiarism. But it's too much of a coincidence for both of those things to happen at the same time. And how would Carolyn's accuser even know that she'd seen the application?"

That was why I liked discussing things with Karen. She'd immediately picked up on a problem I hadn't considered. I pondered it for a moment before responding, "You're right, I hadn't thought that through."

"Of course I'm right. You know I'm always right," she teased.

"I do know that; sometimes my memory just fails." We shared a laugh at one of our standing jokes. Then I got back to her question. "But the answer might be that Monica, the woman on the study section, told the accuser that she'd sent Carolyn the grant."

"That would work," Karen agreed.

"At some point then, I'll obviously have to talk to Monica. Or maybe ORI will do that. In any case, tomorrow's meeting with Carolyn's collaborator could still establish that she's innocent. And we can put these ridiculous accusations to bed."

"Sounds good to me." She finished her wine. "And speaking of bed, why don't we go in and have some of the Thai food that's waiting? Then we can go to bed ourselves, where I think I know how to make you relax and feel better."

I followed her in, my imagination having already skipped over dinner.

CHAPTER 4

picked Roz up at MTRI the next morning, and we headed north on I-95 for the two-and-a-half-hour drive to Orono. Her computational colleague, Todd Lehman, was going to meet us there. She'd already sent him a copy of Carolyn's paper, and he'd promised to be ready to go through a comparison of it and Jackson's grant application when we met with Norwood.

A few miles after we passed through Bangor, we crossed the Stillwater River and reached the campus of the largest university in Maine, notable for being Stephen King's alma mater as well as the flagship of the University of Maine system.

Like most universities, parking for visitors was restricted, and it took some doing to figure out how to get to Norwood's lab in the Department of Chemical and Biomedical Engineering. But once Roz got oriented with campus maps, we found a visitors' parking area near the department in Jenness Hall. Todd was already there, waiting for us in the lobby, so the three of us went up to Norwood's office together.

Norwood was talking to a couple of students when I knocked on the door. Given his attitude when I spoke to him on the phone yesterday, I expected to be told that we needed to wait until he finished. But instead, he greeted me warmly and told the students that he'd have to get back to them later that afternoon.

After I introduced my colleagues, he waved us to seats at a small round table and asked if we'd like him to send out for sandwiches so we could have lunch while we talked. I was grateful for the offer, since it was past noon and I anticipated spending a couple of hours with him, but surprised by his hospitality.

He handed us menus from a pizza and sub shop. "This place delivers, so just let me know what you want, and I'll call it in." Then he smiled at me. "Don't look so surprised, Professor Parker. I'm sorry I was short with you on the phone yesterday. It's just that I didn't know what this was all about, and your call took me by surprise. But Carolyn called later and explained that you were a friend who was trying to clear up some confusion about our newest paper. So no worries, I'm happy to help."

I thanked him as we made our selections, a meatball sub for me, and he placed the order. Then we got to work.

I led off with an introductory question. "What we're specifically interested in is the relationship between the computational analysis you did for your paper with Carolyn and work that Garrett Jackson has done. But it would probably help us to have a little background before getting into the nitty-gritty. Maybe you could start by explaining how your collaboration with Carolyn works."

Norwood said he'd be happy to and began by describing how Carolyn had approached him three years ago to ask if he'd be interested in trying a computational approach to identifying candidate drugs against a cancer-related target she was working on. He hadn't done that kind of work before but thought it'd be interesting to give it a try. When he did, his algorithm identified a handful of candidate drugs, and he sent Carolyn the list. He'd figured that was probably the end of it, but a few weeks later he got an excited call to tell him that she'd tested his candidates, and one was a winner. That led to their first paper together, and he recalled that he'd been pleasantly surprised by the prominent place Carolyn had given him among the coauthors. Not all experimentalists were so generous with their computational collaborators, he noted.

At that point, a knock on the door announced that lunch had arrived, and we took a short break. When he resumed, Norwood went on to tell us how that initial collaboration had continued and grown. He and Carolyn had published two additional papers together, and they shared a grant as coinvestigators. He particularly liked working with her, not only because she was generous with credit, but also because she had excellent judgment in picking targets that were biologically important. In addition to being prompt and careful in performing the appropriate experiments to test the efficacy of whatever candidates he identified.

I thanked him when he finished, and Todd remarked that it sounded like a great collaboration. Then I turned to the immediate topic at hand.

"I'd like to get back to the relationship between your most recent paper with Carolyn and Garrett Jackson's work. Do you know Jackson?"

"I've never met him, but I'm familiar with some of his work. Why?"

I put a copy of the relevant section of Jackson's proposal on the table. "This is part of one of his grant applications. We're trying to figure out how closely related it is to your paper with Carolyn. If I compare the grant with your paper, I can see some similarities, but frankly I can't follow it well enough to know what's important. Todd here is our computational expert, so we're hoping the two of you can go through it."

"Sure," Norwood said. "Let me take a look at Jackson's proposal."

He studied it for a few minutes before he looked up with a grin. "It's interesting. The computational approach he's using is similar to what I generally do. But it didn't work in our latest project, so I did something new. Here, let me show you."

He got up, went to a file cabinet, and returned with a copy of his paper with Carolyn, which he put on the table next to the relevant pages of Jackson's grant.

"Let's start with the paper that Carolyn and I published. We initially used a library screening method that's the same in principle as what Jackson has in his application, although the details of our algorithms are different."

Todd moved around the table so that he was next to Norwood. "Mind if I have a look?"

"Here you go." Norwood put the grant and the paper in front of Todd. "You can see that what we both did was to use the known structure of a target protein to screen libraries of small molecules for compounds that would bind to the protein's surface. Computationally, of course, which is much more efficient than screening a large number of compounds experimentally."

Todd took a few minutes to compare the grant with Norwood's paper. Then he said, "Okay, got it. Your two methods are pretty similar, but that's not surprising since this is a fairly standard approach in the field. And as you say, the specifics of your algorithms are different."

Norwood nodded and continued. "What's interesting, though, is that the compounds it gave us in this study weren't very effective when Carolyn tested them experimentally. So I tried something different. Namely, we used artificial intelligence to predict new drug–protein interactions. And that yielded a novel drug that worked really well when Carolyn checked it out."

He pointed out the relevant section of the paper to Todd, who again looked it over carefully. Then he smiled. "This is an interesting paper. You describe the screening approach first, then the experiments showing that it ultimately wasn't successful, and finally the AI work that was unique and represents the heart of your work."

"Exactly," Norwood said. "It was really neat how well the AI stuff worked out."

"Makes sense to me," Todd declared. "Brad, you okay? Bottom line is that the grant and the paper both have screening approaches that are similar but not identical. And then the paper has a novel AI approach which is what really worked."

I suppressed an urge to jump up and cheer. This was just what I'd hoped for. "You're the expert, Todd. If you're satisfied, I'm good."

Then I turned to Norwood. "Thank you, I really appreciate your taking the time to clear this up for us. Did you ever see this analysis of Jackson's before?"

"I may have. I attend a lot of the same meetings as members of his group, and they probably presented at least some of this. And Carolyn sent me something similar a while ago."

What the hell! My head suddenly started pounding. I wasn't sure that I wanted to know his answer to the next question. But it had to be asked.

"Carolyn? What did she send you?"

"It was a grant proposal from Jackson, and it had something like this in it. I don't remember exactly because it wasn't particularly useful, and I didn't pay a lot of attention. But I should still have it in my email. Do you want me to look?"

"Please." I barely managed to get the word out without choking.

He spent a few minutes at his computer, presumably searching through his messages. Then he turned to me with a puzzled look. "I think it's the exact same thing we were just going through. Here, I'll print it out for you."

A few minutes later, he handed us copies of Jackson's grant application. Together with an email from Carolyn.

The attached looks a lot like what you're working on, so you might find it useful.

The message had been sent from Carolyn's personal Gmail address, shortly after she'd received the illegitimate copy of Jackson's application.

CHAPTER 5

barely managed to hold myself together long enough to thank Norwood and Todd for their help and return to the car with Roz. I'd never in a million years expected this to be the outcome of today's visit. *How could Carolyn have done this?* It just wasn't the Carolyn I knew.

But as much as I'd always believed in her, there was no denying the email Norwood had shown us. I'd had him forward it to me, so I pulled it up on my phone for the third time, hoping to find some indication that it wasn't really from Carolyn. But the address and contact information hadn't changed since the last time I looked at it. They were still the same as those on a recent email I'd received from Carolyn's Gmail account. Nothing to suggest the email to Norwood was a fake.

"What are you going to do?" Roz interrupted my thoughts with the critical question as I was pulling out of the parking lot.

My head was throbbing. But I couldn't escape from the reality of the situation. Nor could I put aside my responsibility as director and ignore the facts.

I swallowed my feelings and forced myself to respond without emotion. "What can I do? I'm going to confront Carolyn and give her the opportunity to resign rather than going through the disciplinary process and being fired. Then I'll need to notify ORI of the outcome."

Roz's answer was prefaced by a sharp intake of breath. "Are you sure, Brad? Carolyn's one of our best scientists. She's never done anything even remotely unethical before. Maybe she didn't realize what she was doing when she sent Norwood the grant. And since Norwood's work was completely independent, it doesn't seem like any harm was done."

"That doesn't matter. And Carolyn knew exactly what she was doing when she sent Norwood a copy of the proposal. She told the reviewer who sent it to her in the first place that it was a violation of confidentiality, and she was going to delete the application. Instead, she turned around and sent it to Norwood using her personal Gmail account, not MTRI email."

Roz spoke softly. "You think she did that so there wouldn't be a copy on our server?"

"Of course. The grant was sent to her on MTRI email, and that's what she used to reply to the reviewer. Why would she have bothered switching to Gmail if not to hide her email to Norwood? Which she also lied to me about yesterday. I just don't see that I have any choice in the matter."

We made the rest of the trip back in virtual silence. Roz apparently recognized that I wanted to be left alone, and I kept my thoughts to myself as I sulked silently. *What the hell was Carolyn thinking?*

When we got back to MTRI, I made a quick stop in my office to tell Anna the preparations I needed her to make for dealing with Carolyn tomorrow morning. She was shocked at what had happened. And at what I was planning to do. But being the capable administrator that she was, she assured me everything would be taken care of.

Then I went home to get a drink or three.

———

Karen only needed a quick glance at my face to know that something had happened. Before I even closed the door behind me, she exclaimed, "What's wrong? You look like you just lost your best friend. Not bad news about Carolyn, is it?"

"I'm afraid it is. The worst."

Her eyes widened, and she reached out to squeeze my arm. "Brad, I'm so sorry. Come sit on the couch, and I'll get you a scotch. Then you can tell me."

Rosie recognized that something was wrong almost as quickly as Karen had. While Karen went into the kitchen, Rosie jumped up on the couch with me and did her best at cuddling and licking to make me feel better. It didn't work, but I appreciated her efforts.

Karen brought the bottle back with her and poured me a good-sized glass. Then she held my hand and listened without interrupting while I told her everything that had happened. When I finished, she sighed and shook her head.

"It's unbelievable that Carolyn would do something like this. I mean, why? She has tenure and she's well regarded in her field, right?"

I nodded glumly. "Who knows why people do crap like this? I guess we don't know her as well as we thought we did."

"What are you going to do? Have you decided?"

I refilled my glass and had another drink before I could bring myself to answer. "Anna is going to call her into my office first thing tomorrow morning. I'll confront her with the email and give her a choice between resigning or going through a termination procedure, which would result in her being fired. I suspect she'll choose to resign, and Anna will have a resignation letter ready for her to sign. And a security guard will be waiting to escort her out."

Karen raised her eyebrows. "Sounds like you've thought this through."

"Just as well to get it over with. Delaying the inevitable won't change anything."

"I know, but I'm so sorry you have to do this. Carolyn's been your best friend at the institute. Mine too."

"There's no other choice."

"No, I can see that. But there's one thing about your visit with Norwood that doesn't seem quite right."

"What? You think he may have used the information in the grant after all?"

Karen shook her head. "No, I think you can trust your guy Todd on the science. What's bothering me is how you said last night that Norwood was reluctant to meet when you first phoned him. But today he seemed happy to see you and even organized lunch for you guys."

"Right, it was quite a striking turnaround. He said Carolyn had called to tell him that I was a friend, so he was happy to help me clear things up."

"But if she told him you were coming, why didn't she tell him not to say anything about her having sent him the grant?"

I was taken aback. *Why indeed?* I thought for a moment and came up with nothing. "I don't know. Could she have warned him, and he showed it to us anyway, maybe to establish his own innocence?"

Karen shook her head. "Doesn't seem likely. If he hadn't said anything about it, he wouldn't have had anything to worry about. Especially since it seems like it was irrelevant anyway."

"Why then? I can tell your detective brain is thinking of something."

"How do you know the email he got was really from Carolyn?" she asked.

"I thought of that, but it was from the same Gmail account she uses for personal correspondence with me. The address and contact information were all exactly the same, nothing that looked like it had been faked."

Karen shook her head. "That's not good enough. A spoofed email can be sent to show up with the same address and associated information as a real one. And unfortunately, that's easy to do. You can just get an app or use one of several available websites."

Could that really be an out? It seemed too good to be true, but it wouldn't be the first time Karen had seen something I missed. "How can we tell then? I had Norwood forward Carolyn's email to me, so it's here on my laptop. Should I pull it up?"

"No, that won't help. We need to see the header information on the original; it won't be included on a forwarded copy. Among other things, the header will include the IP address the email was sent from, which will give us the sender's approximate location."

"Got it. I guess I can go back tomorrow and ask Norwood to let me look at the original on his computer. Can you tell me how to find what we need?"

"Better than that, I'll save you the trip. Why don't I have one of our detectives from Bangor visit Norwood with an IT guy? They can get what we need first thing in the morning, before you meet with Carolyn."

CHAPTER 6

The first thing I did when I got to MTRI the next morning was to tell Anna to postpone the meeting with Carolyn. Maybe, just maybe, Karen had come up with another explanation for what I'd learned yesterday.

Anna said, "God I hope so!" and immediately picked up her phone. I could hear her talking to Carolyn by the time I opened the door to my inner office.

I waited anxiously for Karen's call. Which happily came soon. I could immediately tell from her voice that it was good news.

"My guys got there before Norwood arrived. They were just about to get someone from university IT to let them in and log on to his computer when he showed up. They told him they were concerned that he might have received a fake email, and he was happy to let them check it out. Bottom line, they found the email and got the IP address. Brad, it wasn't Carolyn! It was sent from New York."

An enormous weight lifted from my shoulders. I'd been desperately hoping for this since last night but hadn't let myself think it could be true. Carolyn was innocent after all.

"My God, I can hardly believe it! Karen, thank you. If you hadn't figured this out, I don't know what I would have done."

"My pleasure. I'm fond of Carolyn too. I'm just glad that I was right about it."

I felt some of my usual wiseass humor returning. "Of course you were right. Aren't you always right?"

She chuckled. "Glad you remember. What are you going to do now?"

"Go tell Carolyn the good news. She must be on pins and needles after Anna set up a meeting with me for this morning and then postponed it."

"I'm sure she is; go for it. Then maybe tonight we can put our heads together and see if we can figure out what the hell's going on. Someone went to a lot of trouble to set up a conspiracy that's this elaborate."

I knew what she was thinking. "And who knows what they'll do when they find out it's failed. Maybe I can learn something from Carolyn that'll get us started."

I sent Roz a quick email to let her know what had happened. Then I stopped on my way out to tell Anna that Karen had cracked the case, and she could tear up the resignation letter.

"That's wonderful! I never believed that Carolyn was guilty. Good for Karen! Should I call Carolyn and have her come in so you can give her the news?"

"No. I'm on my way down to her office to talk like we always do. As friends. Be back in a bit."

I could still hear Anna laughing as the door to the hall closed behind me.

———

Carolyn's office door was uncharacteristically shut, so I knocked and waited instead of going in as I normally would. When she answered, it was to ask who was there in a listless voice. When I identified myself, her voice became even more lethargic. "Okay, come in."

Molly gave me her usual exuberant greeting, but Carolyn just stared at me from behind her desk with a worried look. "You must have bad news. I thought you wanted me to come to your office to deliver it."

I went around to her side of the desk and put both hands on her shoulders. "I did. But it's changed to good news now, so I came here to deliver it instead. Thanks to Karen, we can dismiss the plagiarism charges as trumped-up nonsense."

Her expression turned from astonishment to delight as I told her about our meeting with Norwood, my dismay when I saw what was supposed to have been her email, and how Karen had figured out it was a fake. When I finished, she sat quietly for a few moments with her eyes closed. Then she said, "So it's really over? It's been such a nightmare, being accused of something like this. Thank God for Karen."

"I know. But it's finished now. And yes, you can be thankful for Karen. I feel that way pretty much twenty-four seven."

"But why would someone want to do this to me?" Her face darkened. "Who would hate me this much?"

"I was hoping you could help us figure that out. Somebody went to a lot of trouble to set up a conspiracy this intricate. I think it's important for us to nail them before they try something else. Is there anybody you can think of who might want to derail your career?"

She looked at me blankly and shook her head. "I can't imagine anyone doing something like this. I have some competitors, but my relationships with them are generally pretty cordial. I don't think any of them would sink to this level."

"How about Monica? Do you think she was setting this up when she sent you the grant application? She could have sent the fake message to Norwood at the same time."

She shook her head. "Monica wouldn't do anything to hurt me. We're friends."

"Are you close?" I persisted. "How well do you know her?"

"Not that close, I guess. But we've been to a lot of the same meetings, and we always get together over beers or a meal. She's younger than I am, and I've tried to be a bit of a mentor to her. Introducing her to senior people in the field, helping her get invited to places to give seminars, things like that. She's been very worried about getting tenure, and I've tried to support her there too, although I think she's okay now that she got a paper published in *Cancer Treatment*. Anyway, she's always seemed friendly and grateful for my help. Do you really think she could have done this?"

"Sending you the grant was at least a piece of it, and she's admitted to doing that," I said.

"But don't you think sending me the grant could have been an innocent mistake, like she said in her email?"

"That's hard to imagine. If she did, someone else would had to have found out in order to make the plagiarism accusation and send Norwood a copy."

Carolyn sighed as she took a moment to digest that. "Yeah, I see what you mean. Sorry, it's taking me a while to get my head around all this."

"Understandable. The notion that someone would set this all up to screw you has to be hard to contemplate." She rolled her eyes, and I continued. "Well, the only other name we have to go on is Garrett Jackson, the grant applicant. What can you tell me about him?"

"Not much. I know him by reputation, but we've never met. He's quite senior, and some of his earlier work was foundational to the field. He doesn't go to meetings anymore, but I've heard some of his students present work from his lab. His research is related to mine but not directly competitive."

"How about his students or colleagues? Do you have conflicts with any of them?"

Carolyn shook her head. "I don't even know any of them." She paused. "If all you've got are Monica and Jackson's names, how're you going to try to figure this out?"

"Same way I approach most puzzles like this. First thing I'll do is talk it over with Karen. Then I think the next step is to see what Monica Kushman and Garrett Jackson have to say. After that, we'll just have to see where the trail goes."

CHAPTER 7

Karen had just given Rosie her dinner and was in the kitchen when I got home. They both came to the door to greet me, although Rosie's welcome was rather perfunctory compared to her usual exuberance. Just a quick rub against my leg before she raced back to her food bowl.

Karen laughed as she gave me a kiss. "Nice of her to interrupt her dinner to say hello."

"Indeed. Guess I should be flattered that I at least rate a brief break in her food attack."

"You should be. How'd Carolyn react to the news?"

"She was thrilled. And very grateful to you."

Karen smiled modestly. "It's the kind of thing I do; I'm just glad it worked out for her. Did she have any idea who might be behind this?"

"No, that part of our conversation was disappointing. She didn't give me anything new to go on."

"I'm not surprised. She's too nice to have obvious enemies," Karen remarked.

Just then, Rosie came racing back from the kitchen and took a flying leap at my leg. I picked her up for our usual extensive cuddle. When she was finally satisfied, I suggested to Karen that we take her out for a walk on the beach.

"Good idea. And then let's go to Hobbs for dinner while we talk about next moves. I always think better with a nice plate of lobster in front of me."

———

Hobbs Harborside, right on the water at Wells Harbor, was one of our favorite restaurants. Not to mention the site at which Karen and I had gotten engaged. With tourist season a thing of the past, we were even able to get a window table and enjoy a view of the harbor.

We both knew what we wanted—margaritas and lobsters—so when our server came by, we ordered without bothering to consult the menu. When the drinks arrived a few minutes later, Karen took a sip and got down to business.

"So talking to Carolyn didn't give you any new insights into who's behind this?"

I took a long pull of my margarita before answering. The margaritas were so good here that I always ordered them instead of my usual scotch.

"Not really. She filled in a bit of background on the players we know, and I followed that up with some internet searching during the day. Carolyn views Monica Kushman, the woman who sent her the grant, as a friend. Monica's several years younger than Carolyn and turns out to be a faculty member in the pharmacology department at Westmark University. Her record's pretty thin, and Carolyn said she was worried about getting tenure, but she had a recent paper published in a high-profile journal, so that's apparently okay now. Bottom line is that Carolyn's convinced Monica wouldn't have wanted to do her harm."

"Nonetheless, she was responsible for implicating Carolyn in this mess and was positioned to send Norwood a copy of the grant at the same time," Karen pointed out. "Who knows, maybe she resents Carolyn's success. Jealousy can be a strong motive."

Our lobsters arrived before I could respond, and we paused while they were served. Then Karen immediately started cracking a claw and dug in, her full attention focused on the plate in front of her. I let her eat for a few minutes before I tried to continue. Experience had taught me that nothing came between Karen and a lobster.

She looked up after she finished the first claw. "Okay, my urgent lust for lobster is satisfied. I'll be able to pay attention if you want to go ahead."

I watched as she started on the tail. "Your lobster lust still looks pretty urgent to me, but if you say so. It actually doesn't work for Monica to have been the one who sent the grant to Norwood. The fake email came from New York, but Monica was in Washington, where NIH review groups meet."

Karen shrugged. "She could have sent it to someone in New York as an intermediary. Maybe she needed a friend to help her fake the email."

"That's possible. If I were going to try to fake an email, I'd certainly want someone experienced to help me. And I suppose Monica also could have been responsible for reporting the alleged plagiarism to ORI."

Karen looked puzzled. "I thought that would have been the grant applicant, no?"

"Garrett Jackson. He'd be the logical person, but whoever contacted ORI wanted to remain anonymous. The ORI people assume it was either Jackson or one of his colleagues, but it could have been anybody."

"Meaning that Monica could have done the whole thing, with the help of a buddy in New York. Interesting, although we still don't really know about motive. How about this guy Jackson? Is he a competitor of Carolyn's who might have wanted to screw her?"

"Doesn't seem likely, but it's hard to know. He's older, almost eighty, and apparently quite distinguished. Member of the National Academy of Sciences and holds an endowed chair at Columbia. But his work is somewhat related to Carolyn's, and if it's not him, it could be somebody in his lab. Or a collaborator."

Karen finished the last bite of her lobster. "And Columbia's in New York, so Jackson or an associate could have sent Norwood the fake email. Let's look at this from another perspective. What did the perps need to know to set it up?"

I paused to have some more of my own lobster. At some point, I'd have to catch up to her.

"I've been thinking about that. Basically, they'd need to know about Jackson's grant as well as Carolyn's work. Including when the grant was going to be reviewed."

"Okay, that makes sense. Who knew about the grant?" Karen asked. "Monica and Jackson, of course, but anybody else?"

"Probably people in Jackson's lab. It's likely that he passed around copies to his research group, both to get advice and to give his students an overall perspective on the project. Maybe also collaborators or colleagues whom he asked for feedback on the proposal. Other than that, it would just be people involved with the review process at NIH. All the scientists who served on the panel with Monica would have seen the application. And there are administrators and people on advisory committees who might know about it."

"Got it. And how about Carolyn's paper?"

"Pretty much everyone in her field. She's frequently invited to speak at meetings, so she's undoubtedly talked about the work to diverse audiences. And she would have mentioned that a paper was coming out."

I managed to shovel in some more lobster while Karen contemplated that before offering her conclusion. "The limiting factor would have been access to the grant then, which brings us back to Monica and Jackson—or his associates—as the obvious suspects."

"I agree, with Monica clearly playing a central role. I think the next thing I'm going to do is pay Jackson a visit and see what he has to say about all this. After that, I'll talk to Monica. Hopefully, I can shake something loose from one of them."

"Sounds right," Karen agreed. "I wish I could go with you, but I'm not going to be able to get away from MCU for this."

"No, it doesn't rise to the level of major crime business. But I'll keep you posted."

CHAPTER 8

drove down to Logan Airport the next morning to catch a shuttle from Boston to La Guardia. My meeting with Garrett Jackson was scheduled for early afternoon. The plan was to meet with him and then talk to any of his collaborators or students who seemed like plausible suspects. After that I'd return to Boston, spend the night there, and meet with Monica Kushman the following day.

Jackson's office was in Columbia's Herbert Irving Comprehensive Cancer Center, located in Washington Heights. I left extra time for New York traffic, but it turned out to be a quick trip from the airport, and I wound up getting there half an hour early. Which gave me time to stop at a corner delicatessen and enjoy a nice, thick corned beef on rye—a treat that wasn't readily available back home in Maine.

Jackson greeted me warmly when I knocked on his door a few minutes after two o'clock. "Professor Parker, thank you for coming to see me. Can I offer you something to drink?" Pointing to an espresso maker in the corner, he added, "My espresso's quite good. Or we have tea or sodas if you prefer."

He looked exactly like what he was: a distinguished older scientist with unruly white hair, a bow tie, and a Harris tweed jacket. His office was the sort that universities reserve for their most esteemed faculty members, about twice the size of a standard faculty office and elegantly furnished with an oriental rug, a coffee-colored leather couch with matching armchairs, a six-person oak conference table, and an inlaid mahogany desk.

I took a seat in one of the armchairs. "An espresso sounds perfect. And thank *you* for making time to meet with me. Especially on such short notice."

He smiled faintly. "Oh, I have plenty of time these days. And not many people who want to see me. That's the problem with growing old. Everyone thinks you're useless. And, of course, maybe they're right. I'm just not quite ready to admit it."

"I hardly think that. I even understand that your latest grant application was highly rated and recommended for funding. Not a trivial accomplishment with money as tight as it is these days."

He bowed his head in acknowledgment. "Yes, yes it was. Thank you. But it's only for three years and not a large amount, so that probably helped. Just enough to fund my two remaining students until they complete their degrees. I'm going to retire at the end of this year and transfer the grant to one of my colleagues who's agreed to take care of them."

I was impressed. "It's nice of you to have set that up. Not many people would go to the trouble of applying for a grant to support their students after they retire."

"Well, the dean already agreed to provide funding for them, and we put that in my retirement agreement. But I figured I might as well try to do it myself, rather than leaving it to the university. This place has been good to me, and I didn't want to leave it with a debt if I didn't have to."

That was even more impressive, but I decided not to comment further on his generosity. It was time to get down to business. But first, I tasted the espresso. "Mm, this is excellent." I winked at him. "Will you be opening an espresso shop in your retirement?"

He laughed. "No, that's just for me and my friends. I'm planning to move to a small farm in Vermont and spend my time writing a memoir. I've had a long career, and some of my experiences have been rather *interesting*, shall we say? Often in regrettable ways. But I think it might be useful for young people to hear about some of the less-than-ideal things that go on in science. I recall it was Winston Churchill who said, 'Those that fail to learn from history are doomed to repeat it.' But tell me, what can I do for you? I'm sure you didn't come here just to listen to an old man prattle."

The fact was, I'd already learned what I came for. It wasn't hard to see who Garrett Jackson was, which wasn't someone who'd top off a distinguished career by manufacturing allegations of plagiarism. And if he only had two students left in his lab, they probably wouldn't be plausible candidates either. But since I was here, I took another sip of espresso and plunged ahead.

"There is something I wanted to ask you about. It concerns one of my faculty members at MTRI. Do you know Carolyn Gelman?"

"I've never met her. I haven't gone to meetings for a while. But I know her work. She seems very good, publishes some excellent papers. Is there a problem with her?"

"She's been accused of plagiarism—falsely, we've been able to figure out. Someone made totally trumped-up allegations against her."

He grimaced and shook his head. "That's terrible. I despise that kind of behavior, although I've certainly seen it all too often. Just disgusting when one scientist accuses another of such a thing, and it's always for personal gain. Do you know who made these allegations?"

"Not yet. But I fully intend to figure that out."

"I hope you do. Whoever did such a thing deserves a proper come-uppance. But why are you telling me about this? Surely it should be kept confidential."

"Absolutely. And I trust that you'll do so. But I'm telling you because it's your grant application that she was accused of plagiarizing."

His eyes widened. "*My* grant. That's absurd, I can't begin to imagine why she'd even want to do such a thing. Who reported such nonsense?"

"It was brought to me by investigators from ORI, who asked me to conduct an investigation. The original accusation was made to ORI anonymously, but they assumed it came from you or somebody in your lab."

"Which, I take it, is why you've come to see me. Well, it certainly wasn't from me. And I can't imagine it was from one of my students. As I said, I only have two left, and they're young, just working on their PhD research. There'd be no reason for either of them to make false accusations, even in the unlikely event that they knew what ORI was."

I nodded. "I understand. Are there any colleagues you gave the grant to for feedback? Perhaps a collaborator who was responsible for the computational section? That's the part Carolyn was supposed to have plagiarized."

"The computational section?" He snorted. "That's even more ridiculous. We use a database screening approach, which she's also used quite independently. And more recently she's used the new methods of artificial intelligence, which we haven't tried. In any case, the program we use was written for us by a former student in the bioinformatics program. He graduated last year and has a job in industry. And I've written enough grants by now that I don't shop them around to colleagues for feedback anymore."

"So your students are the only ones who knew about the proposal?" I asked.

"Correct. Except for the various administrators who look at grant applications. Our department financial person, the budget people in the university grants office, my department chair, and the associate dean for research. I don't think any of them are plausible candidates, although I suppose you could make appointments and talk to them. And I'd be happy to arrange for you to meet with my students if you'd like."

"Thanks, but I don't think that's necessary." I finished the espresso. "I'm sorry to have bothered you with this, but I'm sure you understand why I had to talk to you."

"Of course. I wish I could help you figure it out."

I stood up and extended my hand. "We'll get there. In the meantime, thank you for your time. And the espresso. I hope you'll send me an invitation to the opening of your coffee shop."

He chuckled. "If I open one, definitely. And I hope to see you at my book signing."

CHAPTER 9

was confident that Garrett Jackson wasn't involved, and I didn't
see any reason to suspect either his students or the Columbia
administrators he'd mentioned. That left Monica Kushman.
Carolyn's feelings aside, Monica was the one who'd sent her Jackson's
grant. There also had to be a coconspirator in New York who'd sent the
fake email to Ian Norwood, but Monica's role must have been central.
Which made my upcoming interview with her all the more crucial.

She'd curtly replied that she was too busy when I first emailed to
ask about meeting. But I was prepared for that and employed a police
tactic I'd learned from Karen—using a pretext, some might call it a lie
—to get through the door. I told Monica that I'd seen her paper in
Cancer Treatment and wanted to talk to her because I thought she'd be a
strong candidate for a faculty position that MTRI would soon have
coming open in her field. Her calendar loosened up, and she was able
to make time to see me the day after my meeting with Garrett Jackson,
as I'd requested. Nothing like a combination of flattery and attractive
bait.

She greeted me pleasantly and ushered me into a small, cluttered
office with no windows and bare gray walls—the kind of office
younger faculty members sometimes found themselves stuck in. Two

visitor chairs in front of the desk were the only available seating, so I took one. We exchanged pleasantries, and I thanked her for making time to see me.

"I'm flattered that you wanted to talk to me about a possible position," she began. "I looked at your website last night, and MTRI seems to be quite an attractive place. But I didn't see anything about an open position. Have you already initiated a search for a new faculty member?"

I didn't like the idea of continuing to lie to her. But that's what I needed to do if I hoped to get at the truth. Reminding myself that Karen had repeatedly told me that cops are permitted to lie to suspects during interrogations, I kept going with my cover story.

"We haven't started advertising it yet, which is why you didn't see anything on the web. But as I told you earlier, we're planning to make a new appointment in the area of drug development. It will be a replacement for Carolyn Gelman, who's going to be leaving soon. Do you know her work?"

Her mouth opened, and she sat bolt upright. If her shock wasn't genuine, she was a damned good actress.

"Carolyn! Of course, I know her work. We see each other frequently at meetings. But I had no idea she was thinking of moving. She's always said that MTRI is a great place."

"Unfortunately, she's run into a bit of a problem. I'm afraid her departure won't be entirely voluntary."

"I don't understand. Are you saying she's going to be terminated? But isn't she tenured? How can that be happening?"

I sighed theatrically. "Yes, she's tenured. But tenure doesn't provide blanket protection from the consequences of unethical conduct."

Monica's eyes widened. "You're saying she's done something serious enough to get her fired? I can't believe Carolyn would do anything wrong. What's she supposed to have done?"

I suppressed a grin of satisfaction. She'd fallen right into my trap. Which it was now time to spring.

"I think you know the answer to that. She's been accused of plagiarizing a grant application. One that the ORI says you sent to her when you were serving on an NIH study section."

She blinked her left eye three times in rapid succession. A tell? Even good actresses had them.

"Nonsense! I did nothing of the sort. Is that why you're here? Not to talk to me about a job, but to accuse me of some kind of misconduct?"

I gave her a cold stare. "Denying that you sent Carolyn the application is a waste of both your time and mine. I was asked to open an inquiry by two ORI investigators who said you'd already admitted sending it to her. They also showed me the emails the two of you exchanged. Lying to me about it now isn't going to accomplish anything."

She took a deep breath and seemed to calm herself. The blinking stopped. "All right. Fine. Like I told the ORI people, I sent Carolyn the grant to get some help reviewing part of it. But if you saw the emails, you know she replied that it wasn't appropriate for her to look at it and deleted the application. I realize that I shouldn't have sent it to her, but Carolyn didn't do anything with it."

"I'd like to believe that. But somebody made anonymous allegations to ORI, claiming that she plagiarized part of the grant in one of her recent papers." I glared at her. "Were you the whistleblower?"

The color drained from her face. "No! Absolutely not. Why would you think it was me? I like Carolyn. I wouldn't make accusations that could hurt her."

Her denial was no more or less forceful than her previous claim that she hadn't sent Carolyn the grant in the first place. But this time, I believed her. And there wasn't any eye blinking.

"Who else could it be? The allegation had to come from someone who knew that Carolyn had access to the grant. Did you tell anyone that you'd sent it to her? Or send it to anyone else?"

She shook her head emphatically, but the blinking started again. "I most certainly did not. Why would I, when it could only get me in trouble? I don't see why you're assuming that whoever talked to ORI knew that I sent Carolyn the application."

"Because that's the only thing that makes the accusation of plagiarism credible. If you hadn't sent it to her, there'd be no grounds for ORI to have taken it seriously."

"I wouldn't do anything to hurt Carolyn," she protested. "We're friends, and she's always been helpful and encouraging to me. I even think of her as a mentor. It's terrible that she's in this kind of trouble."

I believed she felt that way about Carolyn. It fit with what Carolyn had said, and I'd interviewed enough subjects—both with and without Karen—to have a pretty good sense of when someone was telling the truth. Nor did I see any indication of the jealousy Karen had speculated might be a motive.

On the other hand, Monica was obviously lying when she claimed she hadn't sent the grant to anyone else. She had to have sent it to someone in New York, who in turn sent it to Ian Norwood. Maybe that unknown player in New York had also made the anonymous accusations to ORI. In fact, they could be the scheme's principal architect, and Monica could be no more than a pawn they'd somehow managed to manipulate.

That fit my current reading of Monica. But if it was correct, I'd need her cooperation to figure out who that unknown conspirator was.

I could try threatening her to increase the pressure. But I thought I'd have better luck playing on what I believed was her genuine sympathy for Carolyn, even though that meant another lie.

I put on my good-cop hat. "Monica, I believe you when you tell me that you like Carolyn and don't think she's done anything wrong. I feel the same way, but the evidence against her is damning. Unless you sent the grant to a third party who used it to frame her."

Monica started to protest again, but I held up a hand to stop her. "I don't think that harming Carolyn was your intent, but I'm pretty sure you aren't telling the truth when you say you didn't send it to someone else. And if you stick to that story, Carolyn's career is over."

She'd gone white as a sheet and was visibly trembling. "But you're in charge of MTRI. If you believe she's innocent, why don't you just dismiss these crazy allegations?"

"I wish I could, but it's ORI's call, not mine. Without evidence to the contrary, the charges will stand, and I'll have no choice but to fire Carolyn. You're the only one who can supply the evidence that would clear her."

I handed her a card with my contact information. "Think about it.

Her fate is in your hands. If there's anything you want to tell me, call or email anytime."

———

I drove back to Maine, worried that I'd blown it. If Monica didn't respond to my ploy, I didn't know what to do next. But her email came in when I'd been on the road for only about an hour. A quick glance told me it was good news, and I pulled over to the side of the interstate to read it.

*I do have more to tell you. There **is** some kind of plot, and I can't let this happen to Carolyn. A man approached me and bribed me to send Carolyn the grant, and also to send him a copy from a secure account. I didn't know what he was going to do with it, but now I can see it was bad.*

I'll drive up to MTRI tomorrow morning and give you all the details. Will you be available around 10?

I pumped my fist in the air in a solitary gesture of triumph and responded.

Thank you! Tomorrow at 10 is fine for me. But I'm eager to know who it was that approached you.

Her reply was immediate.

Sorry, I don't know his name. I just called him Mr. Black because he wore all black clothing. But I think some of what I can tell you tomorrow may help you figure out who's behind this.

CHAPTER 10

had Anna clear my schedule from nine o'clock on in case Monica arrived earlier than she planned. Then I went down to my lab to check in with my students. I got updated on a couple of experiments in progress and returned to my office a few minutes before ten. No Monica yet, so I tried to concentrate on routine paperwork while I waited.

By the time ten thirty had come and gone, I could barely contain myself. *Where was she?* I was about to call her office and see if she'd decided not to show after all when there was a knock on the door.

I got up to open it with a welcoming smile. But instead of Monica, I was met by two men I'd never seen before, a heavyset man with salt-and-pepper hair and a younger man, tall and thin with a crew cut. They both wore coats and ties.

I thought for a moment that they might be more ORI investigators. But then the older one showed me a badge. "I'm Detective Zelen, Boston PD. My colleague here is Detective O'Brien. Were you planning to meet with Monica Kushman this morning?"

Why were two Boston detectives asking me about Monica? This couldn't be good. My answer came out in a nervous rush.

"Yes, what's wrong? Has something happened to her?"

Zelen delivered the news. "I'm sorry to tell you, she was killed last night. Shot by an intruder."

I recoiled in shock. "She was murdered?!"

"I'm afraid so. Are you okay? We'd like to ask you a few questions if you're up to it."

I took a deep breath. "Of course. I'm fine, it's just that that was quite a shock." I gestured toward my conference table. "Why don't we sit over here?"

When we were seated, O'Brien took over. "Again, we're sorry for your loss. Did you know the victim well?"

"No. I just met her for the first time yesterday. We spent less than an hour together."

"Her calendar showed a meeting with you yesterday. And we found subsequent emails between the two of you arranging another meeting this morning. Can you tell us what's going on?" Zelen asked.

I figured a capsule summary was all they needed. "She sent a confidential NIH grant that she was reviewing to one of my faculty members, who was subsequently accused of plagiarizing the material. I investigated the matter at the direction of the NIH Office of Research Integrity, and it turned out that the faculty member had been framed. I met with Monica to question her about her role."

"And?"

"She admitted sending my colleague the grant but claimed it was an innocent mistake."

Zelen raised a skeptical eyebrow. "Did you believe her?"

"No, I was convinced she was lying. It seemed clear that she was involved in some kind of plot against my colleague."

"Is that the Carolyn she mentioned in the email?" O'Brien asked.

"Correct. Carolyn Gelman."

Both detectives wrote down the name. Then Zelen continued. "In the email, Monica admits there was something going on. And it sounds like she knew Carolyn. Do you agree?"

I nodded. "I made it clear that I didn't believe Monica's denials when I left her yesterday. She sent the email an hour later and was going to tell me the truth about what had happened this morning. She and Carolyn were apparently friends, and I think I made her feel guilty about her role in a scheme that would have destroyed Carolyn's career."

"It certainly sounds like that from the email. *I can't let this happen to Carolyn*, she wrote." He gave me an amused half-smile. "Was making her feel guilty part of your interrogation technique?"

"I figured it was my best chance at getting something out of her."

"It seems to have worked." Zelen nodded approvingly. "Nice move."

"I had a good teacher. My fiancée's commanding officer of one of the state police major crimes units. Karen Richmond, maybe you know her."

"Karen! I worked several cases with her when she was with the FBI in Boston. I remember she joined the Bureau after she worked with a university professor to crack a murder case involving another prof in the guy's department. I guess she likes you academic types; she and the Boston guy were an item at the time. You'd probably know who he was if I could remember his name."

I looked at him with a straight face. "I believe the guy's name is Brad Parker."

It took him a moment to get it. Then he let out a loud guffaw. "You son of a bitch, it was you! And now you got her to come up to Maine and make things permanent. You must be quite a hunk."

I joined in his laughter. "I don't know about hunk, but yes, I'm the lucky guy."

He continued grinning, but his tone turned serious. "I agree, you are a lucky guy. Karen's a good one. But we better get back to work. Do you have any idea what Monica was planning to tell you today?"

I shook my head. "Only what was in her email."

"Or who her mysterious Mr. Black might be?"

"Not a clue."

Zelen sighed. "Okay, I guess that covers it then. Is Carolyn Gelman here? We should probably talk to her too."

"I think she is. I can have my assistant take you down to her office. Do you think Monica's murder is related to these plagiarism charges?"

"Who knows? We're just starting our investigation. But it's certainly something we need to consider."

Both detectives got up and started toward the door. Then Zelen paused. "One more thing. Did Gelman know what you suspected about Monica's involvement?"

"I told her that I thought Monica was part of whatever was going on. She didn't know that I met with Monica yesterday, or that she was coming here this morning."

"So Gelman would have considered Monica to be part of a conspiracy against her? And she wouldn't have known about Monica's plan for a come-to-Jesus visit this morning?"

I wasn't sure what he was getting at. "I guess that's right. Unless Monica emailed her last night too. Why do you ask?"

"No reason," Zelen said. "Just curious."

CHAPTER 11

My phone rang around four, and I was pleasantly surprised to see the call was from Karen. I didn't like to bother her during the day, so I'd planned to wait until tonight to tell her the news. But now I'd go ahead and get it off my chest.

Except she went first. "I understand the meeting you were looking forward to this morning was replaced by a visit from an old friend of mine in Boston homicide, Stan Zelen."

"Sadly so. Monica was apparently shot and killed last night. How did you know?"

"Zelen called me. What do you think happened?"

"I suppose it could be a coincidence, but I have to think it's related to the plot against Carolyn and our meeting yesterday. Maybe the wrong person learned that Monica was coming to see me this morning."

"I agree. It's not a coincidence, and Zelen doesn't think so either. Did you know that they also interviewed Carolyn?" she asked.

"I knew they were going to, but I haven't seen her to hear how it went. Why?"

"That's what Zelen called me about. I'm afraid they consider her a suspect, and he needs an officer from Maine to work with them since they're out of their jurisdiction."

I sat bolt upright. "Carolyn a murder suspect?! And work with them to do what? They didn't have anybody from Maine with them to meet with me."

"She apparently raised some suspicions when they interviewed her. And now he's asked for my help because he can't get an out-of-state warrant. That needs to be done in cooperation with the local authorities," Karen explained.

I saw red. "What the hell! You're helping him take out a warrant against Carolyn! To do what?"

"To search her house. And c'mon, Brad, I don't have any choice other than cooperating with a request from the Massachusetts police. Surely you can see that."

I took a moment to calm down. "All right, I get it. You couldn't refuse any more than I could refuse to investigate her when ORI brought charges to me. Sorry I reacted so strongly. But this sounds pretty drastic. What went on when they talked to her?"

"Unfortunately, enough for them to want to take the case further. First off, she confirmed you'd told her that Monica was involved in a conspiracy to accuse her of plagiarism. She also told them that she'd been exonerated but agreed that those charges threatened to destroy her career, which Zelen and his partner saw as possible motive."

"All right, I can see that. But Carolyn would've been home with her kids last night. When was Monica shot?"

"Between eight and nine. But the kids are in Portland for a long weekend with her ex, so Carolyn went to Boston to have dinner with some visiting scientists. And then she told the detectives that she stopped by to see Monica."

"What! Why the hell would she do that?"

"She told them she just wanted to pay Monica a friendly visit and ask if she knew anything about what had happened. But there was no answer at Monica's apartment, so she came home."

"Jesus Christ!" I exclaimed. "And the detectives think she's the one who shot Monica. But why would Carolyn kill her? We already have evidence exonerating her from the plagiarism charges, and Monica was coming to see me this morning with information that might have cleared everything up."

"Zelen said Carolyn knew you were convinced that she wasn't guilty, but she didn't know you'd met with Monica or that Monica had set up a second meeting for this morning. Did he get that wrong?"

"No, he got it right. I haven't seen Carolyn since I got back from Boston."

"So what they're thinking is that Carolyn decided to question Monica herself," Karen explained. "That went wrong, they fought, and Carolyn shot her. Or so the story goes."

Now I understood why Zelen had asked what Carolyn knew before he left my office this morning. I kicked myself for not having updated her yesterday. "What horseshit! Where's the gun supposed to have come from? Did Monica own a gun? I doubt if Carolyn has one."

"That's not so clear. Carolyn denied having a gun, but there's a twenty-two pistol—which is what Monica was shot with—registered to Carolyn's ex. Zelen's partner contacted him, and he says he left it at the house when he moved out. The gun's one of the items specified in the warrant."

I couldn't believe it. Carolyn had gone from being falsely accused of plagiarism to being suspected of murder. "And what else are they after?"

"Her electronic devices. They want to go over them for any communications between her and Monica."

"They're going to take her phone, iPad, everything? She'll go ballistic."

"I know, but it can't be helped. I'm going to serve the warrant and do the search with them myself. Maybe having me there will make it easier on her."

"I'm sure it'll help," I agreed. "And I'd like to come with you."

"I figured you'd say that, and no doubt Carolyn would appreciate it. But I'm afraid having civilians take part in a search is verboten. And it's Boston homicide's party, so it's not my call."

"Why don't you try asking Zelen? If you tell him I promise to stay out of the way, I have a hunch he just might say okay. The two us sort of clicked this morning."

I could almost hear her roll her eyes. "You think you charmed a hard-boiled homicide detective in a single meeting? Sure, I'll ask. He'll get a good laugh out of it."

She ended the call, leaving me feeling that she was probably right, and I was over-estimating the significance of my interaction with Zelen. But when she called back ten minutes later, her tone had changed to one of amusement.

"I don't know what kind of male-bonding went on between the two of you, but your new best bud says you can meet us at Carolyn's house at seven."

CHAPTER 12

stopped at home to take care of Rosie and grab something to eat, which turned out to be some leftover chili that I heated up in the microwave. Then I headed out for Carolyn's house, about a half hour away in Kennebunkport.

Karen pulled up just as I arrived, and we parked in front of the house, behind a car with Massachusetts plates. Zelen and O'Brien got out as we walked up to them.

"This lady has quite a place," O'Brien observed. "Big contemporary right on the ocean. Must be worth a bundle. I didn't realize you scientists made this kind of dough."

"It's the house she shared with her ex-husband," I explained. "He's a lawyer who can apparently afford it. Carolyn didn't want to upset the kids with a move in addition to the divorce."

Zelen waved a hand impatiently. "Whatever. Let's get to work." He handed Karen the warrant. "We picked this up earlier. It's your state, you take the lead."

The detectives stood behind us while Karen rang the doorbell. At first, Carolyn greeted us with a big smile, but the smile was replaced with a wary look when she saw Zelen and O'Brien. Molly sensed her owner's tension and stood next to Carolyn at full alert, ready to defend her human against whatever threat these two strangers presented.

"What is this? What's going on here?" Carolyn held the door only partly open and asked the question in an angry voice. Molly backed her up with a low growl.

Karen licked her lips and spoke softly, trying her best to be soothing. "I'm sorry, Carolyn, but we have a warrant to search your house, and these detectives have some questions for you. If you cooperate, I'm sure we can make it quick and painless."

Not surprisingly, Carolyn didn't react well. "Search my house! For what? And what the hell are you doing with these Boston cops?"

Zelen stepped forward. "The warrant is for items linking you to Monica Kushman's murder. We need you to please step aside and let us in."

His tone was still mild, albeit more aggressive than Karen's had been. But Carolyn reacted with a loud gasp and a step backward. Molly seconded that reaction by growling and baring her teeth. Coming from the 130-pound Newfoundland, it was a frightening display. Zelen kept his cool, but I saw O'Brien's hand move toward his gun.

I stepped in front of him, putting myself between him and Molly. "Okay, let's all calm down." Then I held out my hand for Molly to sniff. "It's all right, big girl. You know me. We're okay."

She sniffed, stopped growling, and nuzzled the familiar hand. I murmured, "Good girl," in a soft voice. Then I stepped through the half-open door, knelt beside her, and started to pet her. That had the dual effect of calming both her and Carolyn. Molly started to give me her usual tail-thumps and rub her head against my chest. Carolyn took a deep breath and opened the door.

Karen stepped in, followed by Zelen and O'Brien. "Thank you," Karen said. "This shouldn't take long. And I'm sure it'll clear up any questions these gentlemen have about your involvement."

Carolyn still looked wary but seemed to have accepted the inevitable. "All right. What are you looking for?"

Zelen took the lead. "Let's talk for a few minutes first. I'd like to revisit the trip you told us you made to Boston last night."

"Fine. What more do you need to know?"

"You told us you went into town to have dinner with two visiting scientists. Where was that?"

"The restaurant in The Charles Hotel in Harvard Square. Henrietta's Table, I think it's called. You wrote down their names earlier."

Zelen checked his notebook. "Right, got it. And when did you arrive and leave the restaurant?"

"I got there around six. They were waiting in the bar, so I had a drink with them, and then we went to our table. We left a little after eight."

"And what did you do then?"

"It was still early, and I remembered that Monica lived near Kenmore Square. It wasn't far, so I found her address and went to the house. Like I told you, I just wanted to have a friendly chat with her."

"A friendly chat?" O'Brien interrupted. "With the woman who accused you of plagiarism?"

"Brad had already told me that I'd been exonerated. And I didn't believe she was the one who'd accused me, although I thought she might know something."

"And when did you get to her place?" Zelen asked.

"Probably around eight thirty. But there was no answer when I rang her doorbell, so I knocked on the door a couple of times. When there was still no answer, I left and came home."

"Did anyone see you there?"

"I'm not sure. I saw a guy on the street when I pulled up, but I don't know whether he noticed me."

"Can you describe him? And his car?"

"I couldn't see his face. He had a hoodie pulled over his head. About the only thing I can say is that both the hoodie and his pants were black. I didn't see his car either. He was walking toward Commonwealth Avenue when I spotted him."

"Okay." Zelen closed the notebook. "The next thing we need is to borrow your electronic devices. Computer, phone, iPad, anything you have that'll send an email."

Carolyn's lips tightened. "What for? I need those things. And you can see all my emails on the MTRI server."

"Not if they're sent from a private account," Zelen pointed out. "You can have everything back in a day or two."

Carolyn started to protest, then gave Karen a questioning look. When Karen nodded, she acquiesced and handed Zelen her phone. "My iPad's on the table next to the couch, and my computer's in the office."

Zelen gave the phone to O'Brien, who put it in an evidence bag and went over to the couch to get the iPad. Then Zelen asked Carolyn to take us to her office.

She led us down the hall to a room dominated by a floor-to-ceiling window that looked out over the ocean. Her desk was set up in front of the window, strategically placed to give a background view of the rocky coast while she worked. The laptop was on her desk, and O'Brien added it to his evidence bag.

"Thank you," Zelen said. "Now we need to look for your pistol."

"I told you earlier, I don't have a gun."

"Do you want to reconsider that statement?" O'Brien asked. "There's a twenty-two caliber pistol registered to your ex-husband. He told us that he left it here when he moved out."

"I don't know anything about it. I know he had one, but I thought he took it with him. You're not going to tear the house apart looking for it, are you?"

"I hope we don't have to," Zelen replied. "Could you show us which room he used as an office?"

"This one. But it's my office now, and I've cleaned out all his stuff."

Zelen looked around and pointed to a small closet in the back of the room. "Mind if I take a look in there?"

Carolyn shrugged. "Knock yourself out. There's nothing much there. Just a few boxes of stored papers."

Zelen opened the closet door and reached up to the top shelf. He had to stretch, but after feeling around above his head for a moment he pulled down a black metal box. "What's this?"

"I don't know. Maybe Paul—my ex—left it behind. I can't reach up there, so I've never looked."

"Uh-huh. Looks like a gun safe to me. Sure you don't know anything about it?"

"No! I told you, I never saw it before," Carolyn insisted.

"I see. What's the combination to unlock it?"

"How would I know? But Paul didn't like to bother with combination locks or passwords, so he usually just used dumb things like one, two, three, four."

"That's what he told us. Let's try one, two, three, four." He punched in the numbers and opened the box. Then he glared at Carolyn as he held up the open box for her to see. "It's a twenty-two caliber Smith and Wesson, right where your ex said it would be. Anything you want to tell us now?"

Carolyn paled as he spoke. But for good measure, O'Brien piled on. "Like how you took the gun and used it to shoot Monica? You can only help yourself by telling us the truth. Maybe the two of you were arguing and shooting her was an accident. We could understand how that might happen."

"I did no such thing," she protested. "I told you, Monica wasn't even there last night. And I've never seen that box before. Or the gun."

"If you say so." Zelen's disbelief was obvious as he handed the gun to O'Brien. "We'll let ballistics tell us whether this is the murder weapon. The only other things we need for now are your fingerprints and a DNA sample. We can take those here, if you're willing to cooperate. Otherwise, we can go to a local police station."

Carolyn threw up her hands. "I don't care at this point. Go ahead and get it over with."

O'Brien swabbed her mouth for DNA and used a mobile device to take her fingerprints. When he was finished, Zelen looked over at Karen. "We need to talk outside for a minute. Dr. Gelman, please wait here."

CHAPTER 13

Karen followed the detectives out into the hall. I wasn't sure whether Zelen wanted me there or not, but I tagged along anyway. If this was going to be some kind of executive session to review the evidence, I wanted to be part of it.

He closed the door behind him when the four of us were out of the office. "This has become pretty interesting. Gelman was in Boston last night and admits going to the victim's home around the time of the murder. And despite her denial, she had access to a twenty-two caliber pistol."

Karen shook her head. "I'm not so sure about that. She could very well have thought her husband took the gun when he left and never come across it in the top of the closet."

"Possible," Zelen acknowledged. "But ballistics will give us the answer we need. And we'll know more from the lab soon. If the gun was the murder weapon, and we find her prints or DNA at the crime scene, it's a done deal. We're also getting her phone's GPS history, so pretty soon we'll know exactly when she got to the victim's home and how long she spent there."

"Meantime, the evidence is pretty clear," O'Brien stated flatly. "Motive is obvious, she was in the right place at the right time, and she had access to a gun that's consistent with the murder weapon. Since she must have planned to take the gun to Boston with her, we're looking at murder one."

"We still need to canvass the area for witnesses who may have heard or seen something," Zelen noted. "But I agree with O'Brien. This is all pointing in one direction, and I suspect we'll have enough evidence for an arrest soon. In the meantime, Karen, we need you to take her into custody."

That was too much. I exploded, breaking my vow of silence. "What the hell, are you both nuts! Everything you have is circumstantial! And your idea of motive doesn't make sense, since I'd already told her she'd been exonerated from the plagiarism charges."

O'Brien turned toward me, his eyes flashing. "Shut your mouth! You shouldn't even be here. Try to interfere, and I'll put *your* ass in a cell."

"Wait a minute, everyone." Karen kept her voice under control, but her tone of authority was clear. "Brad, you need to stay out of this. But he makes a good point, detectives. Once Carolyn knew she was in the clear, why would she kill Monica?"

"Bullshit. You never heard of revenge?" O'Brien shot back.

"Doesn't fit here," Karen insisted. "Judging from Brad's discussions with her, I don't think Carolyn ever considered Monica to be the brains behind the plagiarism accusations. She might have wanted to talk to Monica to see if she knew anything, but she wouldn't have any reason to kill her. And based on Brad's interactions with Monica, I think there's a better alternative."

"Are you crazy!" O'Brien started to yell at her.

But Zelen held up a hand. "Wait a minute, let's hear her out. Karen, what are you thinking?"

I'd already lost my cool and started to jump in. "What she's thinking is—"

Karen looked at me coldly. "Brad, I'm quite capable of telling them what I'm thinking."

I took a deep breath. "You're right. I'm sorry."

She gave me a forgiving wink before she continued. "Brad was pretty confident after talking to Monica yesterday that she'd been used by a third party in an attempt to discredit Carolyn. The email she sent afterward confirmed that, and she had more information she was going to reveal this morning. Which suggests an obvious motive that third party had for getting rid of her last night."

I couldn't contain myself. "If whoever's behind the plagiarism scheme knew that Monica was about to tell me the truth, they're the ones you should be looking at."

O'Brien had been chafing at the bit. Now he took the opportunity to let his frustration loose. "Damn it Parker, what part of 'stay out of this' don't you understand? C'mon, I'm taking you out of here!"

He started forward toward me, but Karen put a restraining hand on his chest. "Look, calm down—"

But before she could complete the sentence, O'Brien struck her hand away. "Touch me again and I'll knock you on your ass, lady."

Karen responded by hooking her left leg behind his and shoving hard. He fell over backward and hit the floor with a thud. When he looked up at her, she gave him a mocking laugh. "You mean like that? I don't think so. And I'm not 'lady' to you, Detective. You can call me either ma'am or Lieutenant."

He started to get up in a rage, but Zelen stopped him. "Why don't you cool off, you moron? And apologize to *Lieutenant* Richmond."

When O'Brien was silent, Zelen shouted, "Now!"

"All right, all right," he finally mumbled. "I apologize. Lieutenant."

Zelen glared at him for another minute before turning to Karen. "Is that what you think could be going on? That the killer is whoever set Gelman up for plagiarism in the first place?"

"That's who had a motive, not Carolyn. And I don't think it's a reach to think that anyone who could set up a scheme like this could have hacked into Monica's email."

"Maybe. I see where you're coming from," Zelen acknowledged. "Well, between the crime scene investigation, ballistics, and Gelman's GPS history, we'll know more soon. You'll just have to hold her for a day or two before we have enough to either charge her or cut her loose."

Karen shook her head firmly. "No. I'm not going to take her into custody. It's not necessary."

O'Brien couldn't keep out of it. "Why, because she's your friend? She's our prime suspect in a murder investigation, and from the looks of this house, she has the resources to run anywhere in the world."

"She also has two children, a thriving career as a tenured professor, and a big research group. As well as being innocent. She's not going to run. *Detective.*"

O'Brien started to yell at Karen again, but Zelen cut him off. "Watch it!" His tone left no room for argument, and O'Brien was wise enough not to offer any.

Zelen held his eyes for a moment before returning his focus to Karen. "O'Brien may be an asshole, but I agree that we can't give Gelman a chance to run. If you won't hold her on suspicion, will you at least agree to keep her under surveillance? Otherwise, I'm going to have to get the FBI involved. There's too much to just let her go free."

I thought Karen was going to tell him to go to hell, but she surprised me. "Okay, I'll set up surveillance. We'll have eyes on her twenty-four seven."

"And how about tonight, before you get that arranged?" O'Brien asked in a voice laden with sarcasm. "You gonna just leave her loose when we leave?"

Karen gave him a look that shut him up again. But then she capitulated. "All right, I'll stay in the car and sit on her myself until we get a schedule organized."

Zelen stepped in before O'Brien could object further. "That'll work. I'll go tell Gelman we're done for now, but she shouldn't go anywhere without telling you."

He came back out of the office a few minutes later, and we all went to our cars. After the detectives pulled away, I asked Karen if I should wait with her.

She gave me a tired smile. "No, no reason for us both to exhaust ourselves. You've had enough police work for one night. Go home, relax, and take care of Rosie. I'll text you when I have an idea how long it'll be."

CHAPTER 14

poured myself a tumbler of scotch and turned on a rerun of *Law and Order* when I got home. Rosie jumped up on my lap, and we got comfortable to wait for Karen. But then she texted to say she'd be stuck at Carolyn's until around two. Not long after that, I decided to call it a night and took Rosie upstairs to bed. When I finally felt Karen crawl in beside me, it was almost three.

I dragged myself up at my usual six o'clock. Karen was normally awake before me, but this morning she was still snoring rhythmically. She no doubt needed the sleep after last night, so I took Rosie downstairs, gave her breakfast, and made coffee. When it was ready, I filled a mug and took it down to the beach for Rosie's morning walk.

It was a leisurely stroll, with Rosie making several stops to wade into the ocean far enough to get her belly wet and then run back out to the sand. Her idea of a swim. I expected to find Karen up and about by the time we got back to the house, but she was still upstairs. With luck, that meant she'd arranged with her office to be in late. If so, there was no reason I couldn't do the same, freeing the two of us to enjoy a lazy morning together.

With that happy thought, I refilled my coffee, got my iPad, and went out to the deck. The emails that had come in last night were all routine, so I started reading *The Boston Globe*. The lead article in the Metro Section took care of my hopes for the morning.

The article was by an N. Morgan and ran under the headline, "Cancer Research: Plagiarism and Murder." It was a mixture of facts, half-truths, and blatant exaggerations. According to the *Globe*, Carolyn Gelman, a researcher at the Maine Translational Research Institute, had been identified as the prime suspect in the murder of Monica Kushman. Gelman was said to be under investigation for plagiarism and was about to be fired. The article further stated that she believed Kushman, a rival researcher in cancer drug development, was responsible for the career-terminating charges against her and killed Kushman for revenge. A team of Boston detectives and Maine State Police had searched Gelman's home last night, and incriminating evidence was being subjected to forensic analysis. An arrest was believed to be imminent.

I'd just finished reading when Karen came up behind me and put her arms around my neck. "Sleeping in felt good. How'd you like to come back to bed with me?"

That was just the invitation I'd been hoping for. Until the *Globe* article had killed my mood.

"I'd love to. Except for this."

She regarded me quizzically as I handed her the iPad. But as soon as she looked at it, her face hardened. "Shit!"

She took a minute to read it, then looked up with an angry scowl. "Goddamned reporters. They never take the time to get a story right. All they want is to make it as dramatic as possible."

"I guess that's what sells papers," I commented.

"Yeah, I know. But look at that headline. It's overblown, even for them. Is this going to cause Carolyn more trouble?"

"It can't help. I'm sure it'll upset her further. And it's bound to set off a barrage of nasty rumors."

"Do you think she's seen it? Most people up here probably don't read the Boston papers. We just keep getting the *Globe* because we're from there."

"I know, and I doubt if Carolyn reads the *Globe*. But you can be sure that someone who saw the article said something to someone else. And so on and so on. Scientists are great gossips, especially when the news is bad. A story like this is going to circulate quickly at MTRI as well as throughout Carolyn's broader scientific community. It'll inevitably be an embarrassment for her. The stuff about plagiarism as well as the murder crap."

Karen looked at the iPad again. "Maybe you can help with that. The article says that Carolyn was about to be fired for plagiarism. You could call the reporter and let her know that's not true, that your investigation instead established that Carolyn had been framed. You can't comment directly on the murder allegations, but you could cast doubt on the motive by pointing out that Carolyn knew she'd been cleared."

I brightened a bit at that. "Interesting idea. Maybe I can start nullifying some of this. I'll not only contact the reporter, but I'll also send an email to MTRI faculty and staff, as well as our trustees. That should give the rumor mill something different to chew on."

"Good idea." She rewarded me with a kiss on the back of my neck. "It'll make Carolyn feel better too, just knowing that you have her back."

"Which is also important," I agreed. "Where do you think the reporter got the story anyway? She says her source spoke on condition of anonymity. Think it's O'Brien?"

Karen rolled her eyes. "Maybe. But who knows? The Boston PD leaks like a sieve. At least it did when I was there, and I doubt if that's changed. Cops like to curry favor with the news media, and leaking a juicy tidbit like this is a good way to get a reporter in your debt."

I nodded as I got up from the table. "Yeah, I can see that. Okay, I'm going to go draft that email and get it sent off before I go to MTRI. If you can hang on a minute, I'd like to run it by you before I hit send."

I had the email composed in my head by the time I got upstairs to my office, so it didn't take long to get it on the computer and send it to Karen.

Dear Colleagues,

I'm sure many of you have already seen the article about Carolyn Gelman in this morning's Boston Globe. *I'm writing to clarify some of the erroneous information that was reported.*

First, Carolyn is **not** *under investigation for plagiarism and is most* *certainly **not** about to be fired. The truth is, I was asked to conduct an investigation by the NIH Office of Research Integrity because a grant application had been inappropriately sent to Carolyn by its reviewer. I looked into the matter with the assistance of a small faculty committee, and we quickly concluded that Carolyn had done nothing wrong. There was no plagiarism.*

Second, it is important to note that Carolyn was fully aware of our findings. The motivation the article suggests she had for shooting Monica Kushman makes no sense. And while I can't comment directly on the police investigation, I'm confident that their work will likewise confirm Carolyn's innocence.

Thank you for your patience and support for our colleague during this difficult time.

Brad Parker, Director, MTRI

Karen had read the draft by the time I got back downstairs. "Perfect. No need for my edits. But why don't you send it to the *Globe* reporter as well as your MTRI folk? That'll give her a chance to look at it, and you can follow up with a phone call in an hour or two."

"Good idea. I assume the *Globe* has an email address for her."

"I already got it. Her name's Nancy Morgan, email nancy.morgan@globe.com.

"Thanks, I'll go get it sent off. Then I better get to the institute and see what other fires need to be put out. Can I take a rain check on your offer to go back to bed?"

Karen smiled seductively. "I'll look forward to it."

CHAPTER 15

My inbox was full by the time I got to the institute. There were at least two dozen emails from MTRI faculty members, all responding to the message I'd sent out and thanking me for clarifying the situation. And for backing Carolyn. The uniformity of support for her among the faculty was gratifying, as was a short but heartfelt message of thanks from Carolyn herself.

There were also two emails from members of the board of trustees, which I approached with a bit more concern. The first was from James Cameron, the chairman of the board. He expressed his hope that the situation would be promptly resolved in Carolyn's favor and thanked me for my handling of the matter. But he also cautioned me to remain objective and asked that I attend the next meeting of the board's executive committee to review the charges of plagiarism and explain how I'd reached the conclusion that Carolyn was innocent.

The demand to justify myself stirred an initial feeling of unease. But then I decided there was no reason to be defensive. Asking me to explain my actions was not only his prerogative but his responsibility to the institute. And it would be simple enough for me to do.

The second email was from one of my favorite board members. Dr. Isabelle Fisher was a retired neurosurgeon whose husband, Allen, a very successful hedge fund manager, had succumbed to lung cancer several years ago. She was smart, forceful, and a generous donor with a special interest in helping advance the careers of women in science and medicine. She and Carolyn had met last year when I asked Carolyn to give a presentation to the board, and Isabelle had congratulated me on having such an outstanding young woman as a member of the faculty.

When I read her email, I was delighted to see that hadn't changed.

Thank you for your support of Carolyn and your efforts to clear up these ridiculous charges! She's a superstar, and I trust you won't let this nonsense get in her way. Just let me know if you need my help with any of the other trustees.

I smiled to myself. As long as Isabelle was on our side, I had no reason to worry about the rest of the board. None of the others could stand up to her in a fight.

The last message responding to my email came as a surprise. It was from Nancy Morgan, the *Globe* reporter. I hadn't expected to hear from her and figured this would be an angry note telling me I was out of bounds to have claimed that her article contained erroneous information. But that's not what she'd written.

Please call me to discuss your message. Your assertion of Dr. Gelman's innocence is quite at odds with what I was told by a reliable source, and I'd like to get the story straight.

I wasn't sure I wanted to talk to a reporter. Whatever I said, it'd be easy for her to take something out of context and further distort the truth. And what good could come from it? I seriously doubted that she would risk damaging her credibility by printing a correction to the story.

On the other hand, Karen had been the one who suggested talking to her. Meaning Karen must have thought the conversation had the potential of yielding something useful. Maybe I'd do it later.

The last thing in my inbox that interested me wasn't a response to my email, and I didn't think it had anything to do with Carolyn. It was from Martin Dawson, an old friend from graduate school who was now at Yale. Despite the distance, we'd stayed in touch, although the last time I'd seen him was several years ago when he helped with the case that had brought Karen and me together. An adventure that had culminated with the three of us having a memorable dinner at what Martin enthusiastically described as New Haven's finest restaurant. Maybe he was writing to tell me that he was coming up to Maine, and it was my turn to arrange a comparable meal.

I was thinking of Fore Street, one of Portland's award-winning restaurants, as I opened his email. It asked me to give him a call, so I did.

A woman answered the phone, "Dean's office," reminding me of Martin's current position in upper university administration. When I asked if he was available, she replied that she thought Dean Dawson was in a meeting, but she'd check.

A moment later, Martin's voice boomed over the line. "Hey, Director Parker, how you doing?"

I chuckled. "Probably about as bogged down in administrative shit as you are, Dean Dawson."

"It's a bitch, isn't it? We make our reputations by doing good science, and they reward us by sticking us in jobs with so much administration that we can't do our own stuff anymore. The Peter Principle at its worst."

It was always fun to listen to Martin's banter. "Tell me about it. Although I'm still managing to keep my lab going, at least at half-mast. Anyway, I hope you emailed to tell me you're coming up here and we should have dinner. It'd be more fun to commiserate with plates of Maine's finest in front of us. And I know Karen would love to see you again."

"And we could celebrate the two of you getting engaged. I knew that was coming as soon as I saw you guys together!"

Had he really, I wondered? Although a committed relationship with Karen was something I wanted, I was far from sure it would happen back then. But sometimes Martin had a knack for sensing things that others missed.

I was going to pursue it, but he changed direction before I could respond. "Actually though, I'm afraid I called to talk about business. I had dinner with our chair of pharmacology and Carolyn Gelman the other night."

That was a shocker. "With Carolyn? Was it the two of you she met in Cambridge?"

"You sound surprised. Hasn't she told you that we're wooing her for a position down here?"

"I am surprised. She hasn't said anything about it, and she's usually completely open with me."

"Maybe that's to be expected. We haven't made her an offer, just chatted in general terms when she was here a few weeks ago, supposedly to give a departmental seminar," he explained. "It's a high-level position, director of a new center for advanced drug design with an endowed chair in pharmacology, and we've kept it quiet to be sure we don't embarrass any of the candidates. But at this point the search has narrowed, and Carolyn's at the top of the list, so we started talking to her more directly."

"Got it. I saw her after your dinner, but I'm afraid there were other things on her mind."

"I know. That's why I wanted to talk to you. I heard rumors of plagiarism a while ago but figured it was just gossip. Then this morning I saw the *Globe* article."

"What a pile of crap! The so-called plagiarism charges were trumped up." I filled him in on the details, concluding, "Carolyn knew she'd been exonerated and had no motive. The rest of the so-called evidence is circumstantial and I'm sure will evaporate after a few days of investigation."

"That's pretty much what I expected. And I'm glad to hear it, I immediately liked her when we met the first time she visited. We obviously can't proceed with recruiting her at this point, but I'm just going to put it on hold until she's officially cleared. Then, old buddy, I'm going to steal one of your best colleagues."

I laughed. "We'll see about that. She's happy here, and I think I'll be able to keep her."

"Want to bet on it? Maybe a good dinner? This is a pretty fancy position. Director of Yale's new high-tech center, endowed chair, and pretty much whatever she wants in terms of resources."

"You're on. I already have a restaurant in Portland in mind. And I can taste the champagne you'll be buying for us."

CHAPTER 16

told Anna I was going to talk to Carolyn and would be back shortly. Then I went down to her office, wondering if the optimistic front I'd put on for Martin was realistic. Between Yale's prestige and deep pockets, they could put together an offer that would be hard to resist. I was confident that she liked it here, but the question might come down to my ability to match whatever they put on the table. Or at least come close. I suppressed an involuntary sigh as I knocked on her door and went in. All I could do was try.

Molly gave me her usual energetic greeting, but the bags under Carolyn's bloodshot eyes made her look less than chipper. Nonetheless, she managed a smile.

"Morning, Brad. And thanks again for the email you sent out earlier."

"No problem. But how are you doing? You don't look so hot."

She grunted in response. "Being accused of murder does that to a girl. Is there anything new? Do the detectives still think I did it?"

"I'm pretty sure Karen and I weakened their resolve by making it clear that you didn't have a motive, but they still think you might have killed Monica for revenge. At this point, they're continuing to investigate. Hopefully, that'll lead them to someone else soon."

"Do you think it might be the guy I saw in the black hoodie? He could have shot Monica before I got there."

"Possibly. Is there anything more you remember about him?" I asked.

"Unfortunately, no. I didn't get any kind of look at him."

"Well, maybe they'll find something at the scene that'll help. Or maybe a neighbor saw him. Meantime, there's something else I need to talk to you about. I got a call from Martin Dawson at Yale this morning."

Her face fell. "Oh Brad, I'm sorry. I should have told you myself, not let you hear about it from them. But I only realized they were seriously thinking of offering me a job the night before last, when I had dinner with them. They talked to me about it before, but just in general terms about what kind of person would be good to be director of their new center. I had no idea they considered me to be a candidate."

"I figured it was something like that. Don't worry, no harm done," I reassured her.

"I'm surprised Dean Dawson bothered to call you about it. It must be off the table after that *Globe* article."

"We're old friends, and he wanted to get my take on the situation. When I told him the real story, he said something to the effect that he was happy to have been right about you, and they'd just hold off on making you an offer until you were officially cleared."

Her eyes widened in surprise. "I wasn't expecting that! Thank you, getting me out of trouble seems to have become your full-time job. But I'd have thought you'd want them to drop the idea of recruiting me, so I'd stay at MTRI."

"Oh, no question that I want you to stay," I hastened to confirm. "But you've made some major contributions, and it's only to be expected that a first-class place like Yale would want you for a new leadership position. I'm neither surprised nor unhappy that they're trying to recruit you. I just hope that you like it here and decide to turn them down."

"I do like it here, you know that. And I hope you know how much I appreciate your support. In everything. But to be honest, this would be a hard offer to refuse. It's Yale and the position would come with an endowed professorship in pharmacology. It'd also be a big jump in salary as well as a lot of lab space and guaranteed research funding from the university."

"No surprise there. If a place like Yale wants someone, they go after them with everything they have to offer. Plus, there's the prestige of it being Yale. But tell me, if everything else was equal—like the salary and research support—would you rather move or stay here?"

That was the critical question, and I was thrilled when she responded without hesitation. "I'd rather stay here, no question. I'm perfectly happy here, it's just that what they're offering is too good to pass up. Having research funding that doesn't depend on NIH would let me try out some new ideas so I could get the preliminary data I need to apply for grants. And now that I've gotten rid of my idiot ex-husband, the extra salary would really help with the kids. Especially when I think about college coming up fast. Bobby's twelve already, and Gail's just two years behind."

"I'm delighted to hear you say that you'd rather stay here. That makes it my job to put together the resources that'll let you do just that, including what you need for Bobby and Gail."

"How can you? MTRI doesn't have endowed chairs, let alone the kind of salary and research support they're talking about."

I smiled and shrugged my shoulders. "Then I guess it's about time for us to get in the game, wouldn't you say? Seriously, top faculty get offers from other institutions all the time. Their current institution then needs to decide whether to let them go or put together a competing offer to keep them. A retention package, we call it. In your case, the answer is simple—we very much want you to stay. Of course, I can't turn MTRI into Yale, and we don't have a new drug design center for you to be director of. If those are the attractions, there's not much I can do."

"No, I don't care about the institutional prestige, and I'd much stay here than move to New Haven. I also don't really want the administrative responsibility of being a center director. Maybe in a few years, but at this stage of my career, I'd rather keep focused on my research. But they're offering a lot of money, both in salary and research support."

I was starting to think Martin might be buying dinner after all.

Getting someone to move from one institution to another usually required both a push and a pull. If Carolyn was happy here, meaning there was no push for her to leave, the pull would have to be irresistible. For some people, an endowed chair at Yale would do it. But if that wasn't Carolyn's priority, and it came down to resources, I at least had a shot.

"Understood. And you also mentioned they were offering you a lot of lab space. Is that a factor?"

"Not really; you've already given me all the space I need."

"Good. Then what I need to work on is getting you an endowed chair with a salary increase and institutional research funding. What kind of numbers are we talking about?" I asked.

"I can't believe you're considering doing this! Well, the salary isn't set yet, but the range they've mentioned is almost twice what I'm getting now. And they've asked me to develop a budget for the research funding, based on a new project I want to get started. I'm still working on that, but it'll be close to two million."

That was a lot of money, but I wasn't shocked. Yale had deep pockets, and the trajectory of Carolyn's research made her worth the investment. The question was whether I could put together a competitive offer.

"That's quite a package. Yale wants you bad! And we want you to stay here at least as much, so I'll get started working on this."

"Can you really? I didn't expect you to do anything like this."

I spoke with more confidence than I felt. "I'll do my best. Send me your research budget when it's done, and I'll get together with our financial mavens on it. I assume the total can be spread over a few years?"

"Some of it, sure. I'm figuring general research funding for a technician, two postdocs, and supplies for a five-year period. But I also need top-of-the-line instrumentation for analyzing drug–protein interactions from day one, and that's quite a chunk of change when you start figuring in maintenance contracts and operating support."

I suppressed a grin. With everything else going on, I hadn't told her about the new grant yet.

"Well, being able to spread the general funding over a five-year period makes it possible to handle that piece from our operating budget. Let's talk more about the molecular interaction instrumentation. Do you need it for your exclusive use, or would adding it to our shared facilities work?"

"Having it as part of our shared instrumentation would be fine. And I know we have a grant submitted for that, but we both know it's unlikely to be funded. Especially in these days of declining budgets at NIH. And not being able to do that kind of analysis is really a problem. As it is now, I have to send my students to a collaborator's lab in Boston to do the work."

I let the grin show. "Haven't I had a chance to tell you that our grant has just been approved for full funding? I guess things have been so busy—"

"Brad, you're kidding!" She jumped up and threw her arms around me. "That's absolutely wonderful!"

The grant couldn't have come at a better time, I thought. "Figured that'd make you happy. So, if I budget the personnel and supplies funding on an annual basis, does that take care of the research support part of their offer?"

She gave me her biggest smile. "It sure does!"

"Good. I'll need to work with the board of trustees for the endowed chair and associated salary, so send me the figure from Yale when they make you a firm offer. And I'll have to hold off until the cops let you off the hook, too. In the meantime, I'll get started on the budget work and approach a couple of my usual donors on the board to plant the seeds. As soon as the detectives drop the case against you, I'll make sure the *Globe* runs a corrected story and we'll be ready to roll."

Molly gave me an extra nuzzle as I was leaving, which I took as a thank-you. It had probably been a while since she'd seen Carolyn look so happy.

CHAPTER 17

was surprised to find Karen's car in the driveway when I got home and even more surprised to find her and Rosie in the kitchen. With everything that had gone on this morning, we hadn't made plans for dinner, so I'd assumed we'd either go out or get something delivered. Karen cooking was the last thing I expected.

She laughed when I kissed her and said as much. "It was an unusually slow day at the unit, so I decided to take off early. Picked up some swordfish at the fish market and fresh corn at the farm stand. I just started marinating the fish, so we can relax and have a drink."

I kissed her again, deeper this time. "Good plan. I've had quite the day to tell you about."

"I have some news we need to talk about, too." She poured some scotch for me and picked up the glass of wine she was drinking. "Let's sit out on the deck, and you can start. I'm curious about how things went at MTRI."

I followed her out, sat next to her, and helped Rosie get comfortable on my lap. Then I launched into my story. "It turned out to take a totally unexpected turn, which I'll get to in a moment. First, let me satisfy your curiosity. By the time I got to my office, quite a few faculty members had responded very positively to my email, thanking me for clearing things up and supporting Carolyn. She sent me a message expressing her thanks, too."

"Good. How about the others you emailed? The trustees and the reporter?"

"The chairman of the board wrote back, thanking me for sending out the message but also warning me to be objective and requesting that I attend the next executive meeting to explain what was going on."

"That sounds like less than enthusiastic support," she commented. "Are you worried about it?"

"Not really. I'd do the same thing if I were in his position. And I also got an email from Isabelle Fisher. She was totally supportive of Carolyn and even offered to help me with the other trustees if I needed it."

"She's the trustee you really like, right? The one you always say is the smartest and toughest of the bunch."

I took a sip of scotch. "Yep, that's her. She'll have no problem taking care of the chairman if it becomes necessary."

"So far, so good. What was so eventful then? Did you talk to the *Globe* reporter?"

"I haven't talked to her yet, but she also responded to my email. She said it was very different from what her source had told her, and she asked me to call her because she wanted to get the story right."

Karen looked puzzled. "That sounds promising. Why didn't you call her?"

"I partly decided to wait until we heard something from the detectives, hoping that would give me enough to convince her to put the story to rest. And then I opened the next email, which wound up taking over the rest of the day."

She raised an eyebrow. "I take it that's what you meant when you said the day was eventful. But before you tell me, let's get dinner going."

I finished my scotch and followed her into the kitchen, where she started the broiler for the swordfish and told me I was in charge of the corn. Which I liked to microwave with the husk on. "Two ears'll take about six minutes," I said. "Let me know when to start."

"I figure about ten for the fish, so give me a few minutes lead. Can you tell me about the surprise that took over your day while we're doing this?"

"Chew gum and walk at the same time? I don't know, but I'll give it a try. It started with an email from Martin Dawson," I began.

"Your old friend from Yale? The one who took us out for that fabulous dinner a few years ago?"

"That's Martin. And that's exactly the way he'd like you to think of him, too. Nothing's more important to Martin than a good dinner."

She laughed. "I remember that. Did he email you about setting up another dinner? It'd be fun to see him again."

"His email just asked me to call him. When I did, it turned out to be about Carolyn. But to reassure you before I get into it, we ended the conversation with a bet for dinner. He said it would double as a celebration for our engagement, which he claimed to have predicted when he first met you."

"He's too much! Well, dinner will certainly be fun. But what did he want concerning Carolyn?"

Before I could answer, Karen's timer reminded her to take the fish out, and the microwave gave me a beep for the corn. We paused to serve ourselves and take our plates back out to the deck. Then I proceeded to tell her about my talk with Martin and follow up with Carolyn.

By the time I got through it all, Karen had finished eating. I'd been busy talking so was only about halfway through, and Karen was eyeing my remaining corn with interest.

"Still hungry?" I asked.

She smiled. "No, go ahead and eat. You need to catch up, and I'm more astounded than hungry at this point. Do you really think you can come up with a counteroffer that'll get Carolyn to turn down being a center director with an endowed chair at Yale?"

I finished the corn and had another bite of fish before I answered. "I do. I can't match Yale's prestige, but that's not what she cares about. The salary and research support that come with the endowed chair are the important things to her, and I think I can put together the resources to match that part of their package. With some additional funding from the trustees."

"And your friend Isabelle Fisher will help you with that?"

"I'm sure she will. I'll talk to her about it as soon as Carolyn's cleared. Have you heard anything from our detective friends today?"

"Yes, that's what I wanted to tell you about. Zelen called me this afternoon. They talked to her dinner companions, I guess Martin and another guy from Yale, who verified that part of her story. As did her GPS history, which showed that she only spent a few minutes at Monica's apartment."

"Okay, that confirms what Carolyn said."

"True. But it would only take a few minutes to shoot someone, so it doesn't really help."

I grunted and speared the last bite of fish. "How about the ballistics?"

"Inconclusive. They couldn't tell whether the gun they recovered from Carolyn was the murder weapon or not."

"Does that happen often? I thought that kind of forensic analysis was usually definitive."

"A finding of inconclusive is actually pretty common, maybe around a third of cases turn out that way," Karen explained. "Unfortunately, it doesn't help Carolyn. Nor did the woman living downstairs. She and her husband own the house and rent out two units upstairs. There's an outdoor entrance leading up to the rental units, and she heard someone knocking on that door last night. When she looked outside to see what was going on, she saw a woman matching Carolyn's description, whom she then identified from a photo the detectives showed her."

"That all fits with what Carolyn said, although I can see that it doesn't rule her out as a suspect. Are there other witnesses? Anyone who saw the guy Carolyn spotted walking away?"

She shook her head. "You think he's an alternative suspect?"

"Could be. And Carolyn suggested that today, too. If he was the shooter, Monica would have been dead when Carolyn got there. And Carolyn said he was wearing black pants and a black hoodie, which fits what Monica mentioned in her email about the guy who recruited her being dressed in all black."

"True, although black hoodies and black pants are pretty common. But no, the detectives didn't talk to any other witnesses. The woman who rents the unit upstairs next to Monica wasn't home."

"So I assume they're going to hunt her down tomorrow? Maybe they should talk to other neighbors as well to see if anyone else saw black hoodie."

Karen frowned. "I'm afraid not. O'Brien is hot to make the case against Carolyn. Thinks everything fits and there's no need to probe further. Zelen's not convinced, but O'Brien went over his head and talked to an ADA who would love to prosecute a nice juicy case like this. She needs to get clearance from her boss, whom she'll talk to as soon as she can get his attention. Until then things are on hold, and the detectives have been reassigned to investigate the latest gang shooting."

"That's horseshit!" I exclaimed. "Maybe I should go ahead and call that reporter. A different kind of story from her might shake things up."

"No, I have a better idea," Karen said. "Why don't you and I take a field trip tomorrow? Let's see if we can find the witness our Boston friends are too busy to look for."

CHAPTER 18

Traffic was light, so the trip to Boston only took us an hour and twenty minutes. Monica's apartment was on a side street off Commonwealth Avenue, not far from Fenway Park. And just over a mile from our old house in Brookline, which Karen and I bought when we first moved in together.

Google Maps directed us to a yellow Victorian with dark green shutters. Carolyn had told us that the entrance to Monica's apartment was around the right side of the house, but we first went to the front door, hoping to talk to one of the owners. It couldn't hurt to see how well whatever they said to us corresponded to what Zelen had told Karen.

The door was answered by a woman with short gray hair, wearing jeans and a blue T-shirt with *Dog Mom* on the front. She was holding a bichon frisé, who gave out three loud barks and regarded us curiously. When Karen showed her ID, the woman invited us in, introducing herself as Sylvia Odell and the dog as Lola.

"How can I help you? I assume you're here about poor Monica, but I already told the detectives everything I know yesterday."

"I understand, and we're sorry to bother you again," Karen began. "But this is an active investigation, and we have a couple more questions. We understand from the detectives that you heard someone knocking at the outside door leading up to Monica's apartment the night she was shot?"

"Right. Or actually Lola heard the knocking and barked, so I looked out the kitchen window to see who was there. It was the woman I identified for the detectives yesterday."

"Did Monica come down and open the door for her?"

"No. The way it works is that the tenants have an intercom they can use to ask who the visitor is. Then they can unlock the door remotely, and the visitor can go upstairs to their apartment."

"Got it. And did Monica let the woman in?"

"I don't know. I didn't keep watching, just took a glimpse to see what Lola was barking at."

"Did you or Lola see or hear anyone else? Maybe before the woman you identified was here."

Sylvia shook her head. "No, she was the only one we saw that night."

Karen started to thank her and leave, but something was bothering me. Carolyn had told us that she rang the doorbell and then knocked when there was no answer.

I cleared my throat to get Sylvia's attention. "Just one more question before we go. You mentioned that Lola heard the woman knocking on the door. Did she ring the bell first?"

"I don't know," Sylvia said. "The bell just buzzes inside the apartments upstairs. We can't hear it from down here."

———

Karen gave me a grin when we were outside again. "Good catch! I didn't think about Carolyn saying that she tried the bell first."

"It just sort of came to me when we were talking. But if Sylvia and Lola can't hear the bell—"

"I know," Karen interrupted. "The mystery man in the black hoodie could have been there first, rung the bell, gone upstairs to shoot Monica, and been leaving when Carolyn showed up."

"Exactly. And the further implication is that Monica unlocked the door and let him in."

"Suggesting it was someone she knew," Karen observed. "Like her Mr. Black. Let's see if we can find the woman who has the unit next to Monica's upstairs. The woman Zelen said wasn't here yesterday."

We walked around the house to the side door. There were two doorbells, one for M. Kushman and the other for L. Hogan. Karen pressed the Hogan bell, and a few moments later a voice asking who was there came over the intercom. Karen identified herself, we were told to come upstairs, and the door clicked open.

A young woman, maybe mid-twenties, was waiting for us at the door to her apartment. "Hi, I'm Linda. You must be here to ask me about Monica. Poor thing, it's horrible what happened to her. Anyway, I heard the police were here yesterday when I was away, so you must be coming back because I missed them. Come on in and sit down."

We followed her into a small apartment with furniture that looked like college student discards from one of the second-hand shops in Allston. Karen and I sat on a sagging couch in the living room, and Linda brought over a metal folding chair from the kitchen table for herself.

"Were you here three nights ago?" Karen led off. "The night Monica was shot."

"Oh yes, I was here that whole night. Preparing for my interview. That's where I was yesterday, on my first job interview. I'm about to graduate with my PhD in English Lit, and you know how tight jobs are in the humanities. I mean, even if I got this job, it wouldn't be tenure track. Just a visiting assistant professorship. But at least, it'd be a start."

I shot Karen a sideways glance, and she responded with a surreptitious wink. If Linda kept blathering like this, we were in for a long visit.

I tried to appear engaged but at the same time, get her back on track. "I know, it's really tough. Thankfully for my own students, the situation's better in the natural sciences. But we're wondering, did you see or hear anyone visiting Monica that night? Sometime around eight or eight thirty."

"I *did*. I was right in the middle of practicing my seminar. Well, for the third time. Anyway, I heard somebody coming up the stairs. So I looked out through the peephole in my door. I mean, I just wanted to make sure everything was okay. I wasn't spying or anything. Anyway, Monica was waiting and let them into her apartment."

"Did you see what they looked like?" Karen asked.

"Yes, but I don't think it was the same person Sylvia saw downstairs. She said she saw a blond woman, but I'm pretty sure this was a man. I couldn't see his face because he had a black hoodie pulled over his head, but he was at least six feet tall and slender. Once Monica let him in, I went back to working on my lecture."

"Did you happen to notice what time it was?"

"I *did*! Let me just look at my notes." She went over to the kitchen table and consulted a spiral notebook. "It was exactly twenty-two minutes past eight."

I couldn't suppress my surprise. "You wrote down the time?"

"Of course. I told you I was in the middle of my practice talk, and I was keeping track of how long it was. I mean, I had to be sure it wasn't going to take me more than forty-five minutes. Even a minute longer than that, and they'd think I didn't know how to give a lecture. And then I'd never get the job, you know?"

"Yes, I can see it was important for you to remember when you were interrupted," Karen said. She didn't sound nearly as patient with all this blather as I was trying to be.

"Yes, that's exactly it! Then I could keep track of when I started again, and I'd be able to see how long the whole thing took when I finished. I mean, maybe I shouldn't have stopped in the middle, but I had to see who was coming up the stairs. Just to be sure it wasn't an intruder or anything. And my seminar wound up being exactly forty-four minutes. Perfect!"

After a few more minutes of meaningless chatter, we managed to wish her the best of luck in her job hunt and make our escape. When we were back downstairs, I shook my head in mock despair. "Can you imagine what being one of her students would be like?"

Karen sighed. "Unfortunately, I'm afraid I can. One of my chemistry professors in college was just like that. But somewhere in all those words, she told us what we needed to know."

"Indeed, she did," I said. "Our friend in the black hoodie was here before Carolyn. Which confirms her story, right?"

"It does the trick for me. And I think Zelen will get it too. Carolyn's GPS shows her arriving at eight twenty-nine, so everything fits with black hoodie—aka Mr. Black—getting here first, shooting Monica, and being on the way out when Carolyn got here. And with a little luck we may be able to take it further and get a lead on who he is."

"You think we should canvass the neighbors? See if anyone else saw him, maybe without the hoodie or getting into a car?" I asked.

"We could try that, but Carolyn didn't see a car, remember? And if you were going to commit a murder in an area like this, would you drive your car to the scene?"

I thought about that for a minute. Then I saw where she was going. "No, you're right. There are too many people around, and I wouldn't want to risk someone seeing my license plate. I'd take some kind of public transportation."

She nodded approvingly. "That's what I think too, Professor. And we're only a short walk from Kenmore Square."

I finished her thought. "And the Kenmore T station. Where they have video cameras."

CHAPTER 19

We started walking down the street in the direction of Commonwealth Avenue, but Karen stopped when we got to her car.

"What are you doing?" I asked. "It'd be easier to walk than to find a parking space closer to Kenmore Station."

"It would be, but we're not going to the T station. The MBTA Transit Police maintain all their videos centrally, so we need to go to their department headquarters on Southampton Street. It's about twenty minutes from here, near BU Medical Center. You drive, and I'll call Zelen on the way. We'll need his help since I don't have jurisdiction in Massachusetts."

She put the phone on speaker and called Zelen's cell number. When he answered, she got right to the point.

"You need to get back to work on the Kushman case. Brad and I just finished interviewing the homeowner and the woman who lives in the other apartment upstairs. The one you guys missed yesterday. Carolyn's not your killer. The one you want is the guy she saw in the black hoodie."

She went on to give him detailed summaries of our interviews. When she finished, his response was unequivocal. And furious.

"Son of a bitch! I told O'Brien and that idiot ADA that we needed to interview the gal upstairs before deciding to pin this on Gelman. What you're figuring is the black hoodie guy arrived first, rang the bell so the lady downstairs didn't hear, and was seen by the neighbor upstairs at eight twenty-two. Gelman arrived seven minutes later and saw him leaving after he'd shot the victim. She rang the bell, but nobody was alive to answer, so she knocked, and the landlady saw her. That about right?"

Karen said, "You got it," and Zelen exploded with fury. "Goddammit, makes us look like rookie idiots! At least it's you and Parker who figured this out, not some asshole defense attorney who'd rub our noses in it."

Karen gave me a thumbs-up. "Happy to help. We think black hoodie probably used the T, rather than driving. So we're on our way to transit police headquarters—"

"To see if they have him on video in Kenmore." Zelen finished her sentence. "Good idea. You'll need me to get access, so I'll meet you there. Right after I call the moron ADA and put her head straight."

Zelen was already waiting when we reached our destination, so the three of us went in together. When he showed his badge and explained that we needed to view some video from Kenmore Station, the desk officer asked us to wait while he got an investigator to help us. A woman with short red hair came over a few minutes later, introduced herself as Sergeant Wolfe, and led us to a room with a computer console and a half-dozen screens mounted on the wall.

"Kenmore Station, right? About what time are you looking for?" Wolfe asked.

"We figure the guy we want arrived between eight thirty and eight forty-five," Zelen replied. "Wearing a black hoodie, so he should be easy to spot."

"Sounds good. I'll start at eight twenty and fast-forward triple time. Holler if you see something."

It took just a few minutes before a figure in a black hoodie entered the station. Wolfe reversed the video and slowed it up so we could see the time.

"Eight forty-two," Karen noted. "Just about right to walk from the apartment."

"Yeah. Unfortunately, asshole's got the hood up so we can't see his face," Zelen remarked. Then he asked Wolfe if she could keep following him.

We watched him deposit a token in the turnstile, proceed through the station, and board an inbound train. With the hood up and shielding his face the entire time. Then Wolfe switched cameras, and we saw him take a seat off to the side by himself, stay on through several stops, and get off at Park Street downtown. One more camera switch, and we watched him exit the station and melt into a crowd of pedestrians. Hood on and face hidden.

"Afraid that's all I got." Wolfe turned off the video. "Nothing you can use for facial recognition, but I hope it helps."

———

Zelen shook his head when we were back in the parking lot. "It isn't going to help very damn much. We've got this guy on video plus two witnesses, and all we know is that he hides his face under a black hood."

"How about the crime scene?" Karen asked. "Anything there?"

"Nothing. No prints, no DNA. The guy's a pro."

"Well, at least you're looking for the real killer now," I put in. "I assume Carolyn's in the clear at this point?"

"Yeah, she's no longer a suspect. I called the damn ADA on my way here and got my head chewed off. She'd just met with her boss, who gave her the green light on arresting Gelman. Now she's going to have to go back and tell him it wasn't Gelman after all." He chuckled. "Somehow, she didn't think that would get her a lot of brownie points."

"I can tell you're heartbroken over that," Karen quipped. "Maybe it'll teach her to be a little more cautious next time."

"Maybe. Can't say I really give a shit. From my standpoint, the only good thing about this mess is that I'm getting a new partner. I've had it with O'Brien."

Karen grinned and gave him a thumbs-up. "Congratulations. Can't help but be a change for the better."

"That's for sure. I suspect I'll be working with you a bit, too. Both of you, in fact. Although Gelman's no longer a suspect, she's obviously central to whatever the hell's going on."

CHAPTER 20

Karen and I drove back to Maine in silence until we passed the halfway point and crossed the state line into New Hampshire. Then I finally voiced the question I was stuck on. The question I was pretty sure was occupying her mind as well as mine.

"How the hell are we going to get this guy if all we know is he was wearing a black hoodie? And that's only step one. We also have to figure out who hired him. That's the one we really want."

She sighed. "I know. But the only way I see for us to find the boss is to get our hands on black hoodie and force him to talk. If we're lucky, something could still turn up at the crime scene. And I'm sure Zelen's checking whatever cameras he can find around Park Street station. Maybe there'll be more video that'll show us something useful. Like a face or a license plate."

"I'm not thrilled with waiting for news from Boston, are you? They haven't exactly led the way so far."

"I can't argue with that, but I'm afraid I don't have any better ideas. Do you? I'm happy to push forward if you have something in mind."

That put the ball squarely in my court, and we went back to driving in silence while I tried to think of something. Without success. Until Karen's phone rang. As she answered, she mouthed, "Zelen."

"What have you got?" she asked. "Brad's here, and I'm putting you on speaker, okay?"

"We got footage of black hoodie about a block from the T station. Good news is he'd removed the damned hood, and we could see his face."

"Well enough to try facial recognition?"

"The Feds already did. His name's George Evans, and he's well-known to them as a freelancer for hire. Former member of British intelligence, MI6 I believe. Currently living in New York. Wearing all black clothing is his trademark. I'm texting you his picture and vehicle info. I've got guys out canvassing the area around Park Street, and the Feds are looking for him in New York. Shouldn't be too hard to pick up his trail."

"Excellent, nice work!" Karen had a big grin on her face. "I assume you're also looking at traffic cam video and checking the airlines?"

There was a moment of silence. Then Zelen answered in a voice brimming with sarcasm. "Gee, thanks. I never would've thought of that."

"All right, sorry!" Karen laughed. "Keep me posted. Now that you've identified him, it shouldn't be long before either you or the Feds track him down. And remember, we need him alive."

"Roger that. He may have gotten a heads-up though. My idiot ADA went public without any warning and gave a press conference. Probably trying to cover her ass. Announced that Gelman was in the clear and a new suspect had been identified by a witness at the murder scene. The papers are already starting to post it online. Just have to hope that it doesn't scare Evans off before we get our hands on him."

While Karen finished her conversation with Zelen, I pulled up the *Globe* on my phone. Sure enough, a new article on the case had just been posted. It was titled "Break in Cancer Research Murder" and authored by Nancy Morgan, the same reporter who'd written the original. This time, she started off by saying that she'd been informed by the director of Gelman's research institute that the allegations of plagiarism against her had been investigated and found to be baseless. Moreover, the district attorney's office had just announced that Gelman was no longer implicated in Monica Kushman's murder.

Instead, the police were actively pursuing a new suspect whom a witness had identified at the scene.

I got a momentary chuckle out of being used as a source without ever having talked to her. But then a more serious concern struck me, and I turned to Karen.

"The article in the *Globe* online says that the new suspect was ID'd by a witness at the murder scene. Do you think Evans will assume that refers to Carolyn?"

Her eyes widened as she turned to me. "Shit! He probably saw her drive up when he was leaving."

"And even if he didn't recognize her, he could've noticed the Maine plates on her car. He had his hood up, but what if he's worried that she somehow got a glimpse of his face?"

Without taking the time to answer, Karen grabbed her phone, punched in a number, and asked to be put through to Dick Lowe.

I'd met Lowe at a couple of social events. One of the two sergeants in Karen's unit, he was a seasoned veteran whom Karen relied on to function as her second-in-command. When he answered, Karen quickly laid things out.

"Hey Dick, we have a priority situation. Get a BOLO out ASAP for a George Evans. I'll send his photo in a minute. He's a suspect in the Boston murder of Monica Kushman, armed and very dangerous. He may be after Carolyn Gelman, and I need units on her immediately. She's probably at her lab at the Maine Translational Research Institute in Wells. Also, get eyes on all traffic video and set up checkpoints at the relevant exits from I-95 coming up from the south. Just to be safe, make it Kittery, York, Wells, and Kennebunk. He drives a black Mercedes E-class sedan with New York plates, but he'll probably be in a rental."

She paused and I could hear something indistinct being said on the other end of the line.

"Yes, he'll almost certainly resist arrest and have to be taken by force," she replied. "But, if at all possible, I need him alive. I can't make a corpse talk."

When Karen finished and was texting Evans's photo, I called Carolyn to let her know what was happening. To my surprise, she didn't answer her cell. I figured she might be at a seminar, so I called her lab number. This time, one of her technicians picked up.

"She left a little while ago," the tech said. "Something about having to go to a play at the kids' school. And then there was going to be a pizza and ice cream dinner afterward."

I held up a hand to signal Karen. "She's not at MTRI. Left early for a kids' play and school dinner thing."

She quickly turned back to her phone and got reconnected with Lowe. When he was on the line, she told him there was a change of plan. "Gelman's already left her lab for a kid thing. Evans may still go there, so cover it. But send units to her kids' school as well. I'm going to her house in Kennebunkport, so send backup there too."

Then she turned on her siren and pressed down on the accelerator.

CHAPTER 21

The backup Karen requested hadn't arrived when we got to Carolyn's house, so we parked in the driveway and walked up a well-groomed path to the front door. We couldn't tell if Carolyn and the kids were home yet—if they were, she'd have parked in the garage—so we rang the bell and waited. When there was no answer, Karen suggested that we let ourselves in and make sure everything was okay, so I opened the door with the spare key Carolyn had given me for times she was away and needed me to take care of Molly.

At first the house seemed empty. But then I saw a man I recognized as George Evans sitting on a couch facing the door. He was probably fortyish, with neatly trimmed black hair to match his trademark black clothing. He didn't fit my picture of a hired killer except for the gun in his right hand, which was pointed squarely at Karen and me.

Evans's brow furrowed as he looked at us. "You're not the Gelman woman. Who the hell are you?"

Karen didn't miss a beat. "You're correct, I'm not Carolyn Gelman. I'm a state police lieutenant. And you're George Evans. If you want to walk out of here alive, I suggest you drop the gun and get down on your stomach. There are backup units on the way, and they'll be ready to come in shooting."

He gave a harsh snort. "You'd like that, eh? But I don't think so. Why don't you take out the weapon I can see on your hip and drop it to the floor, instead. Nice and slow, just using two fingers." Turning to me, he added, "You do the same."

"I'm not armed." I raised my shirt so he could see, and he nodded. "All right. Don't make any dumb moves."

He returned most of his attention to Karen as she complied with his orders. When she'd dropped her gun, he told her to kick it over to him and show him her ID.

He looked at it with a raised eyebrow. "Commanding officer of major crimes, no less. How impressive. And who's your unarmed friend?"

"Brad Parker," I answered. "Director of the institute where Gelman works."

His eyes lit up. "So you're the one Kushman was about to spill her guts to."

I figured our best shot was to keep him talking. Maybe I could keep him busy until Karen's backup arrived. "And I take it you're the Mr. Black she mentioned."

"That's me. I guess she was rather taken with my taste in clothing."

"Apparently. How much money did it take to get her to betray her friend?"

He shook his head. "It wasn't money. The boss didn't think money would do it. What she wanted was help with her career. Some kind of secure job in research. Boss told me just what to offer, and when I put that on the table, I could see we had her."

"Did you also do the computer stuff? Fake an email to send off with the grant to Norwood and hack into Kushman's account?"

He smiled, apparently proud of his skills. "Sure, that was me. I learned that kind of stuff when I was in the Brits' foreign intelligence. Not hard when you know what you're doing."

He seemed to like talking about himself, so I tried playing on his pride. "Not something just anybody can do, though. And it was important, right? Reading her email was how you knew you had to kill her before she blew the whole scheme."

"It was actually the boss who saw the message she sent you. He wanted to monitor her emails himself, so that's how I set it up. When he saw what she was planning, he called me with the kill order."

"Your boss sounds like a smart guy. He must be to have put together a scheme like this. Who is he?"

I thought for a minute that he was going to tell me. But then he emitted a mocking laugh. "You think you're a smart guy too, huh? Did you really think you could trick me into telling you his name? Of course, it wouldn't matter. You're both dead anyway. And we may as well get it over with."

I knew that would be coming sooner or later and had been watching Karen out of the corner of my eye. As Evans pointed his gun at my chest, she bent her legs, preparing to jump him. Maybe if we went at him together, we'd have a chance. Albeit a slim one.

But then we heard sirens and looked out to see two cars in the driveway with their lights flashing. Four men got out and ran toward the house with guns drawn.

"Shit!" Evans exclaimed. "Looks like I need a hostage or two." He turned away from me, grabbed Karen by the arm, and dragged her over to the window, keeping his gun pressed into her back.

Holding Karen tightly in front of him with an arm around her neck, Evans shouted at the approaching cops. "I have your lieutenant and a civilian in here. If you want them to stay alive, you need to put down your weapons and back away. Then I'm going to borrow one of your cars and take my two friends here for a little drive. If you boys behave, I'll let them go once we're far enough away."

It wasn't a bad plan, especially for him to have come up with on the spur of the moment. Except he obviously wasn't going to let us go and might well shoot the cops on his way out. I didn't know whether the cops had the same concerns, but they put their guns on the ground and started to walk backward toward their cars.

I figured that now, while Evans's attention was elsewhere, was the best chance I'd get to take a run at him. The odds of success still weren't good, but it was all we had.

But before I could act, he pushed Karen back toward me and turned away from the window, so we were both covered by his gun. The only question was whether he was about to shoot us now or wait till later.

Then a bullet shattered the window, and Evans fell to the ground.

CHAPTER 22

My immediate thought was simple. *We're still alive.* But I knew Karen wanted Evans to stay alive too, and she was already kneeling beside him. I raced over, first to make sure Karen hadn't been injured, and then to help her render whatever aid she was trying to provide.

It didn't look good. Blood was spouting from a hole on the right side of his chest, and he was unconscious. But he was still breathing. I grabbed a pillow from the couch and pressed it into his wound. Once I had the pillow in place, Karen jumped to her feet and ran to the bathroom to get some towels.

While I attempted to stop the bleeding, Evans momentarily regained consciousness and tried to speak. It was barely audible, but I was pretty sure he muttered, "Goddamned asshole professor."

Then he lapsed into unconsciousness again as Karen came running back. And a bunch of cops and an EMT crew burst into the room.

The EMTs immediately took over, putting Evans on oxygen and applying pressure bandages to the wound. Then they got him onto a stretcher and out to an ambulance.

One of the cops filled us in. "They'll try to stabilize him in the ambulance and get him to Maine Medical in Portland. It'll take them about half an hour. If they're not comfortable with how he's doing, they'll take him someplace closer, probably the hospital in Biddeford, until he's stable enough for the trip. Hopefully, they can keep him alive for you."

I realized the speaker was Dick Lowe, her sergeant, as Karen looked up with a grateful smile. "Thanks, Dick. How'd you pull all this off? Pretty impressive operation."

"Just trying to give you a hand, boss. When you said you were coming here, I figured this is where the action would be. And just in case, I brought someone who knows how to shoot along. My buddy James here was a sniper in Afghanistan."

Karen gave him one of her high wattage smiles. "Thanks for being here, James."

"Just happy I was able to help, ma'am."

"Your car was already in the driveway when we got here," Dick continued, "so we snuck a peek inside to see what was happening. When we saw Evans had a gun on the two of you, James got into position, and I called for an ambulance. Then we turned on the sirens to make some commotion. And you know the rest."

"Dick told me you wanted him alive for questioning, ma'am," James said. "I tried to hit him off center, but it was a tough shot, and my priority had to be saving you. I'm sorry if I killed him."

Karen waved a hand in dismissal. "Don't worry about it. You did what needed to be done, and I'm grateful." Turning to Dick, she added, "Do you think he'll make it?"

"The EMTs said it was a toss-up. They'll let us know when they get him to a hospital."

"All right, I guess we just have to wait," Karen said. "In the meantime, let's start cleaning up."

It felt like forever before Dick's phone rang. He listened for a few minutes, then thanked the caller and asked them to call Karen when there was more information.

Then he turned to Karen with a frown. "He's still alive, but there's been severe blood loss and it's touch and go. I guess the good news is they started a transfusion and managed to stabilize him in the ambulance, so they took him to the trauma center in Portland. He was rushed into surgery, and someone'll call you when they know more."

She nodded glumly. "I guess that's something. Can you guys finish up here? I need to let Carolyn Gelman and the detectives in Boston know what's happened."

I followed Karen as she went into the kitchen to have a quiet place away from the cleanup. "Want me to call Carolyn while you call Zelen?" I suggested. "She'll have a heart attack if she comes home with the kids and finds her house full of cops."

"Good idea. It'll probably take a minute for her to get her head around everything."

This time, Carolyn answered her phone. "Hi Brad, I just saw that I missed an earlier call from you. Sorry, I've been at a school concert followed by a pizza and ice cream dinner. What's up?"

"Your tech told me. How's your stomach holding out?"

"Been better, but nothing a few Tums won't fix."

"Well, Karen and I have had a busy day. From the way you sound, I'm betting you haven't heard the news from Boston."

Her tone immediately turned serious. "No, I haven't. Do the detectives still think I'm a suspect?"

"Not anymore. It was the guy you saw in the black hoodie. Who turns out to be a former member of British intelligence. Now a freelancer named George Evans."

I gave her a summary of the events of the day. After an early, "Oh my God!" when I told her that the upstairs neighbor had seen Evans at Monica's apartment, she listened silently. Or at least I thought she was listening. When she still didn't say anything after I finished, I started to wonder if we'd been disconnected.

"Carolyn? Are you still there?"

"Oh, sorry! Yes, I'm still here. Just trying to get this all straight. You think this guy Evans was hired by whoever tried to frame me on the plagiarism charges? And then he killed Monica to stop her from talking to you?"

"Right. Evans was the one who manipulated Monica to frame you. He hacked into Monica's computer and his boss saw the email she sent me."

"And now he was trying to kill me because he thought I'd seen his face at Monica's? But he knew he was hidden under his hoodie."

"We think he saw the news reports, which said a witness at the murder scene identified him. That must have made him think you'd been able to see his face."

"Jesus! Thank God, it also sent you and Karen racing to my house. This guy Evans survived being shot?"

"As far as we know. He was badly wounded but still alive when the EMTs took him. We're hoping he stays that way, at least long enough to tell us who hired him."

"The bastard who wanted to discredit me at the start of all this," she muttered. "I've been racking my brain trying to think who that might be."

"And?"

Carolyn sighed heavily. "Not a clue, I'm afraid. It doesn't make any damned sense."

Karen had finished her call to Zelen by the time I got off the phone with Carolyn. When I summarized our conversation, she nodded. "Zelen's now focusing on the same question Carolyn's wrestling with. He'll have guys search Evans's home and go through his computer, phone, financial records, anything that might yield clues. But that's a long shot, and I'm afraid his bottom line is the same as mine. If we're going to get whoever's behind this mess, I need to squeeze his name out of Evans."

And for that he needs to stay alive, I thought.

CHAPTER 23

I t had been a long day, and our exhaustion was heightened by anxiety over Evans. When Karen and I finally got home, we took care of Rosie, poured drinks, and fixed a quick dinner of leftover roast chicken. We were too on edge to do anything but wait nervously for the call from Maine Med. But we had no idea when it might come, and we eventually dozed off on the living room couch.

To be awakened by Karen's phone.

She grabbed it and looked at the caller ID while I was still trying to figure out what the noise was. "Maine Medical," she whispered, as she put the call on speaker and identified herself as Lieutenant Richmond.

"This is Dr. Rob Aaronson. I'm the surgeon who operated on George Evans, who I'm happy to tell you is alive and stable."

I breathed a sigh of relief as Karen exclaimed, "Oh thank God! I need to question him as soon as possible."

"I'm aware. And he may be up to that by tomorrow. He was lucky that the bullet passed through his body without hitting any major organs. There was, however, a large amount of bleeding, and his biggest problem was loss of blood. It's a damn good thing the EMTs were there at the scene. Their quick action in getting a transfusion started in the ambulance saved his life. Once we got him into surgery, I was able to repair the damage, and he should be fine. He'll be in critical care overnight, but if all goes well, we'll move him to a regular room tomorrow morning, and you'll be able to talk to him. I'd suggest you call around nine or ten to check on progress."

The answer to what had seemed like an intractable puzzle might be no further away than tomorrow morning. I held Karen without either of us saying anything until, in a few minutes, her even breathing indicated she was drifting off again. This time I got her upstairs to bed, and we both fell into a deep sleep.

Karen was still snoring when I woke up the next morning, so I took Rosie out for a quick walk on the beach. Then we got in the car and went to Congdon's to pick up doughnuts, our favorite breakfast.

A fresh pot of coffee was ready when we got back, and Karen was out on the deck. "I was hoping you guys went to get doughnuts," she greeted us. "Grab some coffee, and let's see what's in the box."

I'd gotten two honey dips, two crullers, and two apple fritters. Karen and I both started with honey dips, which not unexpectedly were fresh and delicious. When we finished, Karen announced, "Apple fritter next. But first I'm going to call the hospital. It's eight thirty; close enough to nine for me."

When an operator answered, she identified herself and asked to speak to Dr. Aaronson. Then she listened for a moment and said, "Yes, please have him call me as soon as possible. It's concerning George Evans."

"Aaronson's off duty," she explained after she hung up. "A Dr. Lowenstein is in charge now and he'll call soon. I hope."

It only took about ten minutes, or one apple fritter, for him to call. Karen put the phone on speaker.

"Good news," Lowenstein reported. "He's doing well, and I'm transferring him to a private room. He should be settled later this morning, and you can question him then. Let's say sometime after eleven. Just keep it short and sweet so you don't tire him out."

I gave Karen a kiss when she ended the call. "Looks like you're going to get your chance at him after all. Congratulations!"

"I can hardly wait. Meantime, we have nearly two hours before it's time to leave for Portland. Do you remember that leisurely morning we almost had a couple of days ago?"

"The one I had to take a raincheck on?"

"That's the one. Want to make your claim?"

"Sounds like a fine way to celebrate," I said, eagerly following her back upstairs to the bedroom.

———

We got to the hospital around eleven thirty. A bit later than planned, but Karen agreed that the delay had been worth it. There was an information desk in the lobby, so we stopped and asked where we could find George Evans. The gray-haired woman behind the desk, probably a hospital volunteer, told us he was in room 324, which she explained was in the east wing.

Just as we turned away from the desk, the public address system blared. "Code Silver, third floor east! Code Silver, third floor east! Initiate lockdown procedures. Initiate lockdown procedures."

Karen's eyes were wide as she gasped, "Code Silver is an armed intruder. Let's go!"

We ran toward the stairwell as the lobby began to fill with cops and security personnel. An officer stopped us just before we reached the stairs, but he waved us on when Karen flashed her badge, and we raced up to the third floor.

The east wing nursing station was surrounded by uniforms, again a mixture of hospital security and Portland police. I stayed close behind as Karen pinned her badge to the front of her shirt, pushed through the crowd, and asked one of the cops what was going on.

"A nurse saw a stranger coming out of 324. When she asked who he was, he pulled a gun, shoved her into the room, and tied her up in the closet. By the time she got loose, he'd run off. If he's still in the hospital, we'll find him, but my bet is he's long gone."

"And the patient? The patient in 324?" The desperation in Karen's voice was unmistakable.

"I'm sorry, ma'am, he's dead. Smothered with his pillow."

CHAPTER 24

We stayed at the hospital long enough to convince ourselves that the intruder was nowhere to be found. All the nurse had seen was a man in scrubs wearing a surgical mask. She was able to describe him only as white, dark hair, average height and weight. It would have been easy for him to lose the mask and scrubs and nonchalantly walk out of the hospital before the alarm had been sounded, an explanation given credence by the finding of discarded scrubs and a surgical mask in the trash can of a men's room on the second floor.

The sight of George Evans's remains being wheeled away brought the curtain down on our hope of a resolution. The only thing I could think as we drove back to Wells in silence was, *What the hell do we do now?*

I finally voiced that out loud, without any real hope that Karen would have an answer. She didn't surprise me with one, but she did have some thoughts for next steps.

"Without Evans, I guess we have to go back to trying to figure out who might have wanted to mess up Carolyn's career in the first place."

"And would have been willing to kill to do it," I added.

"That too. I thought I saw Evans trying to speak when I was coming back from the bathroom. Did he say anything?"

"Just something like 'asshole professor.' I think that was referring to his boss, although he could have meant Carolyn or me."

Karen nodded. "I'd bet on the boss, although it doesn't tell us anything new. It was already obvious that whoever set this up is a scientist. He just had to be able to access the dark side to hire Evans. And whoever killed him."

"Unfortunately, it doesn't seem like hiring criminal help would be too hard for most scientists to manage," I remarked. "It could be a competitor, someone Carolyn's hurt or offended, or possibly a disgruntled colleague or former staff member. Only problem is, neither Carolyn nor I can think of anybody who would feel stepped on or threatened by her. Certainly not enough to do this."

"I know. But I think you and Carolyn should try brainstorming again. She's very successful in her field, right?"

"Absolutely. So much so that Yale's trying to steal her for a big-time job."

"You'll be able to handle that, don't worry. But my point is that you can't be a big success without making enemies. Even if you don't know you have them."

"Fair enough," I agreed. "But scientific competitors are one thing. Enemies that would concoct a plagiarism plot and then add in murder-for-hire are another. But sure, I'll get together with Carolyn and see if we can come up with any possibilities."

"Good. And I've got one to throw into the mix. How about the two assholes who were trying to take her down when you first went to MTRI?"

I slapped my forehead. "Jesus Christ, how could I not have thought of Heller and Carlson!"

Maybe the answer was that it had been a long time ago. The institute was in turmoil, the director had resigned, and I'd been asked to step in as interim director to manage the crisis. The problem was that Carolyn was up for tenure, and her case had generated bitter controversy among the faculty. But when I reviewed her file, I couldn't see why there was an issue. She had a strong record of publications and funding, with an important clinical trial in progress. A package that I thought was clearly above the tenure bar. So why were a substantial number of faculty strongly opposed?

It didn't take me long to figure out that Tom Carlson, one of MTRI's most respected and well-funded scientists, had mounted a vicious campaign of disinformation to discredit her. I intervened and made it clear to Carlson that I wouldn't tolerate such conduct. But then things went from bad to worse, and the crusade against Carolyn turned into sabotage of the clinical trial she was running. When two of her patients were poisoned, Karen became involved.

It took a while to sort it out, but it turned out that Mark Heller, a protégé of Carlson's, had collaborated with a pharmaceutical executive to fake data needed for FDA approval of a new drug. Carolyn was on the verge of discovering their fraud, and they'd coopted Carlson and then sunk to sabotage and murder to stop her. By the time it was finished, the pharma exec was dead, Heller and Carlson were under arrest, and Carolyn—now vindicated—was a tenured professor.

"Heller and Carlson," I repeated. "I don't know how I overlooked them. It's not like fraud and murder happen every day at MTRI."

Karen looked at me with an amused smile. "They are kind of hard to forget. Although I didn't think of them right away either, so don't kick yourself. Anyway, Heller's locked up in a federal pen for at least the next ten years, but could Carlson be a possibility? He turned state's evidence and never faced criminal charges."

"He's certainly a candidate," I agreed. "We decided that he wasn't part of the fake data scheme, just a dupe Heller and the pharmaceutical company used to get Carolyn out of the way. Stupid and unethical, but not criminal, so I forced him to resign his position at MTRI and left it at that. I'm sure he hates Carolyn enough to do her whatever harm he can manage."

"Do you know where he is now?"

"No, I have no idea what he did after I fired him. I made the whole affair very public, so I don't think he'd have been able to find another job in research."

"I remember. But whatever he's doing now, it sounds like we should pay him a visit. It shouldn't be too hard for me to track him down."

CHAPTER 25

Two days later, we boarded a plane for Tampa. Carlson had moved to Florida, where he was living in the Tampa Bay area. Karen thought our best move was to show up unannounced, so she'd contacted the local police to establish that he was in town. They verified that he was, and we were on our way to Florida for an overnight.

The Tampa weather apparently didn't realize it was September, and the temperature was still in the upper eighties. Combined with the humidity, it felt overwhelming when we stepped outside the air-conditioned terminal to get our rental car, but luckily it only took a few minutes for the car's air conditioning to kick in. As long as we kept it going full blast, I thought we'd probably survive the half-hour trip to our next air-conditioned destination, Carlson's condominium.

We took I-275 from the airport across Tampa Bay and into St. Petersburg where we turned onto Pasadena Avenue toward St. Pete's Beach. To my surprise, I spotted a flock of small green parrots in the trees on the side of the road, maybe twenty all together. I'd heard about these wild parrots in Florida before but never seen them. They'd originated from escaped pets and were found throughout the state, with St. Petersburg being one of the places they were particularly abundant. A colorful introduction to Carlson's neighborhood.

His address on Brittany Drive turned out to be a gigantic concrete high-rise on the waterfront. My immediate thought was that being on the water would be nice, but calling this place home would be like living in a hotel. Or an institution.

A security guard stopped us at the front entrance but left us alone when Karen showed her badge and explained that we needed to pay a surprise visit to one of the residents. We took an elevator to the twelfth floor and emerged into a dimly lit hallway with a sign indicating that 1232 was to the right. All very much like a hotel. I knocked on the door, and when a voice asked who was there, Karen held her badge up to the peephole. We'd decided she should take the lead because Carlson probably wouldn't recognize her.

"Police," she announced. "We have a couple of questions for you."

A man wearing shorts and a T-shirt opened the door. I wouldn't have recognized him if I hadn't known it was Carlson. He was a shadow of his former self, some twenty pounds lighter with thinning hair, hollowed cheeks, and black bags under his eyes. I would have guessed the man before me was in his mid-eighties, not the roughly seventy-year-old I knew him to be.

On the other hand, he recognized me immediately.

"You! I never thought I'd see you again." He laughed thinly. "I don't suppose you've come to apologize for ruining my life."

Karen held up her badge again and answered before I could say anything. "May we come in? We'd rather talk inside than out here where your neighbors can hear."

As if to emphasize Karen's point, a woman came out of a unit two doors down and looked at us curiously. Carlson opened the door, motioned us in, and crossed the room to sit on a couch looking out over the water.

We sat on a couch opposite him, and Karen was about to begin questioning, but he surprised me.

"I'm sorry, I shouldn't have said that about ruining my life. You were just doing your job. And I deserved to be fired after what I did to that woman. What was her name?"

A repentant Carlson? I glanced over at Karen with a questioning look. Then I answered. "Carolyn Gelman."

"Yes, Carolyn. She didn't deserve to be slandered and bullied like I treated her. No, I shouldn't have done that. Is she still at MTRI?" he asked.

"She is. She's actually been quite successful."

"That's good. I keep thinking I should write her an apology. Maybe now that I know she's okay, I'll be able to."

I didn't bother telling him that Carolyn couldn't care less. Instead, I muttered, "That would be nice."

"Yes, I should do that." His voice had a hollow tone, like he was talking to himself about something that would never happen. "I didn't do very well after I left the institute, you know. I looked for another job for a while, but everybody knew what had happened, and nobody would hire me. Then I started drinking. A lot, I mean. If I drank enough and had some pain killers, I could pretty much forget everything. I hardly even cared when my wife left me. But then I got into a pretty bad accident. Thank God I didn't kill anybody, just smashed my car into the side of a building. But I'd been stopped before for drunk driving, and this time they gave me a choice between rehab or prison. I went into rehab for six months. I hated it, but the judge was right. I got dried out, joined the program, and I've been sober for almost three years now."

"I'm glad," I offered, just to say something and show I was listening.

"Yes, thanks. Anyway, then I moved down here. It's not so bad. The waterfront view's beautiful, and there are a lot of guys like me here. Friends of Bill, I mean. We hang out, play cards, and we even have a dedicated room in the basement for AA meetings. I do that twice a day now. But I've been rambling. What is it the two of you came here to see me about?"

I didn't have anything to ask him anymore. This was a different Carlson. A broken shell of his former self. Barely coherent, but mellow and seemingly repentant. Not the man we were after.

Karen was looking at me though, and I had to say something. "We were wondering if you'd had any contact with Gelman after you left MTRI. Have you followed her work at all?"

"No, I don't pay any attention to science anymore. Not since I stopped drinking. It just gets me upset, thinking about how life used to be. But I'm happy you said earlier that she's doing well."

———

"What's the matter?" Karen asked when we were back in our car. "It's not the answer we wanted, but we learned what we came for. He's not our man."

"I know. It's just damned depressing, seeing what a wreck he is. He was once an outstanding scientist, a leader in drug development. And now he's reduced to a recovering alcoholic living in semi-isolation."

"And you feel guilty about it?" As usual, she'd read me correctly. I grunted agreement, and she shook her head. "You shouldn't. What happened to him was his own damned fault. If you hadn't dealt with him, he'd have destroyed Carolyn's career. He deserved everything he got. In fact, he's lucky to be living in a condo on the water instead of being locked up with his buddy Heller."

I sighed. "I know you're right. It's just depressing to see anybody like that."

"Well, I have something planned for dinner that'll cheer you up. Columbia Restaurant in Ybor City."

I cocked an eyebrow. "Sounds like you've done some homework. I've heard of Ybor City. It's sort of like Tampa's old town, founded by cigar manufacturers in the late nineteenth century, if I remember correctly."

"You've got it. And now it's full of restaurants, bars, and night-clubs. The Columbia is the oldest restaurant in Florida and famous for Cuban food."

I beamed my approval. "Lead on. Just thinking about Cuban food has me feeling better."

The Columbia Restaurant was in a Spanish-style building, deco-rated with hand-painted tiles, that occupied an entire block on Ybor City's main street. Having started as a corner saloon in 1905, it was now the largest restaurant in Florida, with fifteen dining rooms and seating for seventeen hundred. And it was still family owned and operated, the current owner being the great-grandson of the original founder.

We were seated in the Don Quixote room, which Karen had requested at the front desk because she said it fit my inclination for pursuing impossible quests. Like the one we were on now. The room had a turn-of-the-century Spanish feel and featured colorful tiles portraying Cervantes's lead character. I tried softly singing "The Impossible Dream," but Karen hushed me with the comment that the only impossible dream was the idea that I could sing anything on key.

I was thinking of giving it another try, but a waiter came by with menus, and we ordered a pitcher of mojitos. Then I opened the menu and was thrilled to find that Cuban black bean soup was featured. I'd had it a couple of times when I was in Miami for cancer research meetings and loved it, but it wasn't something you could get in Maine—or even, for that matter, in Boston. Karen had never had it but was game to try after hearing my accolades. Choosing an entrée was harder, since the menu featured several tempting paellas and a variety of fresh Florida fish. After some discussion, we wound up going with grouper topped with crabmeat.

The mojitos came quickly, and the soup followed not long after, served with white rice and chopped onions. One taste and I no longer felt bad about Carlson. He was living where he could get this on a daily basis. Plus wild parrots. What more could anyone want?

I dug in steadily and was almost finished when Karen interrupted with a laugh. "Looks like you're enjoying the soup."

"You could say that," I answered with a grin. "Do you like it?"

Her response was to show me her empty bowl. "No, mine really sucked. Do you think we should order another bowl so I can try it again?"

I was about to take her up on that when the waiter arrived with our entrées.

The grouper was exquisite, and the mojitos were perfect for washing it down. We were almost finished before Karen brought us back to business.

"If we rule Carlson out, there's only one person I know who hates Carolyn enough to be behind this. Carolyn's ex."

I raised an eyebrow. "That's interesting. He's certainly enough of a bastard. And he's a criminal lawyer, so he'd know how to hire someone like Evans. But whoever set this up had to be familiar with how NIH works and have the connections to arrange some sort of research job for Monica. Paul doesn't have that kind of background."

"True, but he's at a big law firm. They probably have at least a couple of lawyers who work on patent law and biotech issues. Maybe Paul was able to get the information and contacts he needed from them."

I was doubtful. But who knows? "I guess that's possible. Should we talk to him?"

"No. He knows we're close to Carolyn, and I don't think he'll cooperate if the two of us try to interview him. I'll have a couple of my detectives do it instead. They can just go in saying they want to get his thoughts on any enemies Carolyn has who might be behind this."

"Makes sense," I agreed. "In the meantime, I'll try talking more with Carolyn. Maybe the two of us can put our heads together and come up with some additional candidates."

"Good," Karen said. "And here's another thought. I remember you mentioning when we had dinner at Hobbs last week that people at NIH would have known about Jackson's grant. Could someone like that have manipulated Monica?"

"Maybe. Everybody on the study section with Monica would have seen it, and there are several higher-level advisory committees whose members have access to information on submitted grants. One of them could certainly have seen that Jackson had an application being reviewed by Monica's study section."

"Could you figure out who those people are then? Maybe try running their names by Carolyn and see if any of them might be out to get her."

CHAPTER 26

started by going through Carolyn's personnel file when I was back in my office. Maybe there was a letter of complaint or some record of an incident that I'd forgotten. Possibly something that seemed trivial to Carolyn but could have been magnified in the mind of someone who felt aggrieved.

It was an interesting journey into the past. Her file was thicker than most, which gave me pause at first. But then I realized it was packed with five-year-old complaints from when Carlson and Heller had waged their campaign to discredit her. Other than that, there was nothing unusual, just the normal record of committee assignments, annual reports of grants and publications, progress reports on her students, and occasional notes acknowledging her service on grant review panels and journal editorial boards.

Having struck out there, I turned to people associated with NIH. First I pulled up the roster of the study section that had reviewed Jackson's grant. Then I started compiling a list of members of the relevant higher-level NIH committees. Fortunately, the information was readily accessible on a website that listed all of the more than a hundred NIH advisory committees and their membership rosters. It was an intimidating number at first, but I was able to narrow it down to a half-dozen committees with purviews that were relevant to Jackson's grant. Between them, there were just over forty members, most of whom were well-known scientists. I didn't recognize any of them as being particularly related to Carolyn, but I printed out the membership lists for her to look at.

I tried to be optimistic as I walked down to Carolyn's office. Maybe if we talked it through, the two of us could come up with something, or maybe she'd recognize someone on the study section or one of the NIH committees. At least it would be interesting to see what she thought of Karen's idea that her ex might be a possibility.

After the customary petting session with Molly, I briefed Carolyn on our meeting with Carlson in Tampa. When I finished, she shook her head as if trying to clear it.

"So, the nasty old bastard became an alcoholic, and now he's mellowed out. I guess that's good, although I can't say I give a rat's ass about getting a note of apology from him."

"I didn't think you would. But the point is, neither Karen nor I think he's the one behind this. Frankly, I don't think he has the brain power left to pull it off."

"No, it doesn't sound like it. Any other ideas? I've been trying, but I can't come up with anybody except his buddy, Mark Heller. And being in prison seems like a pretty good alibi."

"Karen had one thought, but first let's see if you and I can come up with any other possibilities," I suggested. "Is there anyone in your field whom you've had a conflict with? Maybe over a race to publish first and claim priority for something. Or competition for an award."

"No. I've never been in a publication race. And you'd know if I'd been short-listed for an award. Hasn't happened."

"I'm sure the awards will come," I said. "But okay, how about someone whose paper or grant you negatively reviewed? Or maybe wrote a negative letter regarding their promotion or tenure?"

She took a moment to think about that. But then she shook her head. "Again, not really. I've written critical reviews of papers, of course, but I always try to make them constructive by specifying what needs to be done to satisfy my objections. Revised versions have usually come back addressing my criticisms, and sometimes thanking me for the helpful comments. Grants are more difficult to judge, but I can't think of a case where an applicant would have had a particular problem with my review. And I always find a way to focus on something positive when I'm asked to write about someone's promotion."

I decided it was time to shift gears. This wasn't getting us anywhere. "All right let's try a different angle. If someone manipulated Monica into sending you Jackson's grant, they had to have known it would be reviewed by her study section. The only people with access to that information, besides Jackson, would be other people on the study section or members of the relevant NIH advisory committees. Could you take a look at those rosters and see if any of them might be candidates?"

I handed her the printouts, and she spent a few minutes reading through them. Then she shook her head with a discouraged look.

"I know some of these people, of course, but none of them are direct competitors, and I haven't had substantive interactions with any of them. Certainly nothing that would have provoked the phony accusations. Sorry, I'm not helping much, am I?"

"No, it would have been easier if you'd made a few enemies," I teased. "But seriously, is there anyone you've had a run-in with here at the institute? Not just other faculty, but maybe a staff member or a student."

"Nothing serious. You know me, I'd rather compromise than fight. I'm afraid the only person I know who hates me enough to have done this is my dear ex-husband."

I raised an eyebrow. "That was Karen's thought, too. But Paul doesn't know enough science to have set it up. Although Karen suggested there might be other lawyers at his firm who could have filled that gap."

"I think she's right. I know there are a couple of former academics there who decided to go into patent law instead of continuing in research."

"Interesting. Well, Karen's going to have a couple of detectives talk to Paul, so we'll see what they turn up. Meantime, if anything else comes to mind—anything at all—give me a holler."

I got up to leave, but Carolyn stopped me. "While you're here, do you have a few minutes to talk about something else?"

"Sure, what's up?"

She handed me a letter. "I got this from Yale, as well as a call from Dean Dawson. He apologized for taking so long and explained that he had to wait until the allegations against me had been dismissed. Now that everything's cleared up, they've officially offered me the job."

I sat back down and read the letter. The terms were the same as Carolyn had told me earlier, including a salary that was more than twice her current compensation. "Congratulations, again," I said. "This is quite an impressive offer."

"Thanks, I appreciate you saying that. I'm going to turn it down, of course. Just thought I'd give you a copy of the letter. There's no way I'd even consider it, not after everything you and Karen have done for me."

"I'm glad to hear that. But this is an important career opportunity, and you should consider it on its merits, not mixed up with personal gratitude. And then, of course, I hope you turn it down because you want to stay here, and we made you a great counteroffer."

She waved a hand in dismissal. "What you outlined previously in terms of research support would be terrific if that's still possible."

"Of course it is. And I also said that I'd get the trustees to endow a chair for you with a salary to match Yale's offer."

She almost blushed. "Oh, you don't have to do that. It's too much. The equipment and funding for my research would be plenty."

I shook my head. "C'mon Carolyn, stop negotiating against yourself. Or have you forgotten those kids of yours who need to go to college? As director of the institute, it's my job to do the best I can to match an outside offer that's threatening to steal a faculty member we want to keep. That would be you."

"All right. But if you can't—"

I held up a hand. "Uh-uh, none of that *if I can't* crap. I know just who to go to on the board of trustees to help me make this happen."

Her eyes widened. "Wow. Well, thank you. I don't know what else to say."

"My pleasure. When are you supposed to respond to the offer?"

"The dean asked me to give him a call once I had a chance to review the letter, so I'll go ahead and let him know I've decided to stay here."

I shook my head. "No, don't do that just yet."

"I don't understand. What do you want me to say to him?"

"For now, just thank him for a very generous offer and let him know that you've shared it with me. You need to give me some time to respond, but you'll get back to him with an answer as soon as possible, hopefully within the next two weeks. Does that sound okay?"

She cocked her head to the side with a puzzled look. "If that's what you want me to do, sure. But I don't get it. Why wait? I've already decided, and it doesn't seem fair to string him along. He seems like a really nice guy. He's also a friend of yours, right?"

"Martin? Yes, he's both a nice guy and a good friend. But you don't have to worry, he'd understand exactly why I'm asking you to hold off for a bit. I just need a little time pressure to make sure my counteroffer sails through the trustees without getting stalled in the budget committee or some such nonsense. Martin's a master of moves like this."

"Okay, now I got it," she said. Then she smiled. "I'm glad to hear he'll understand. I liked him too much to do anything that would cause him trouble."

CHAPTER 27

emailed Isabelle Fisher a copy of Carolyn's offer letter as soon as I was back in my office, together with the terms I wanted to propose as a counter. I was sure she'd be impressed and ready to pull whatever strings were needed to get the board to cough up the funds to endow a chair with a matching salary. Which she confirmed immediately by return email.

Brad, this is quite an offer. It's a credit to MTRI—and to you—for Yale to come after one of our faculty members like this. I'll get to work on the trustees to ante up the chair and salary. More soon.

Good. With Isabelle on the case, I could put the matter of Carolyn's retention aside and turn my attention back to the question I'd originally gone to her office to talk about. We hadn't come up with any new candidates, but I decided that what Carolyn had said about the patent lawyers was worth texting Karen.

Met with Carolyn. The only person she could come up with who hates her is Paul. And she confirmed your thought that there were lawyers at his firm who were former researchers, now specializing in patent law.

Her response was quick.

Thanks for the update. My guys just finished talking to Paul. So far, they like him for it.

I got up from my desk and walked over to the window. Maybe Paul was the answer. The detectives must have learned something incriminating from interviewing him. And he was certainly enough of a bastard to be the guy we were after. His verbal diminution of Carolyn's accomplishments had been nonstop, punctuated by episodes of physical abuse when she stood up to him. If he'd somehow gotten the necessary science information from one of his colleagues, he could be it.

A satisfying image of Paul sitting in Karen's interrogation room came to mind. He was confused and sweating, pummeled by our questions into a state of near incoherence. I wanted to use my fists to finish extracting a confession, but Karen held me back.

It was a pleasing fantasy that was interrupted by Anna knocking on the door. "You have a call from Isabelle Fisher. Do you want to take it?"

I left my daydream behind and answered the phone. Isabelle must be working fast.

"I got in touch with our erstwhile chairman of the board and briefed him on Carolyn's situation," she said. "It wasn't hard to get him on our side, that letter from Yale speaks volumes. He thinks the rest of the trustees will fall in line, with the possible exception of one or two grumblers who won't matter. Can you come to a special trustees' meeting to present the case?"

"Of course, whenever you need me. This is my highest priority."

I could hear the laughter in her voice as she responded. "With this much money on the table, it damn well better be!"

She hung up before I had a chance to thank her, which we both knew wasn't necessary. She wanted to ensure that Carolyn stayed at MTRI nearly as much as I did.

The thought crossed my mind that I might have a free hour to go down to my lab and think about science for a change. But I had to put that aside when an email from the chairman of the trustees himself popped up in my inbox.

Dr. Parker,

Isabelle Fisher has informed me of your proposed counteroffer to Carolyn Gelman. After due consideration, I have decided to support your efforts.

Gelman's ability to attract such an offer from Yale speaks highly of her and would make her retention a big win for the institute.

I'm confident that I can persuade a majority of the other trustees to vote in favor of allocating the resources you request. However, before talking to anyone else, I need your unequivocal assurance that an attempt at Gelman's retention will be successful. I'll have to expend considerable political capital to get the board to approve your package, and it would be a significant embarrassment if she were then to go to Yale after all.

I thus need you to send me an email, suitable for forwarding to the other trustees, confirming that you have discussed the terms of your proposed counteroffer with Gelman, and that she has agreed to stay at MTRI. As I'm sure you understand, I need to be sure we'll be successful before moving forward.

James Cameron

My reaction to his email was about the same as I usually felt when I interacted with James Cameron. What a pompous asshole! And how typical for him to be more concerned with his "political capital" than with the best interests of MTRI. But he was the boss, and I needed his support. Besides, it would be easy enough to respond to his request. After which, I reminded myself, he said he'd approve the package and could get the support of the other trustees. Which would mean I'd succeeded—with Isabelle Fisher's help—in pulling off Carolyn's retention.

I sat back and allowed myself to imagine a world in which both keeping Carolyn at MTRI and unmasking the man behind the plagiarism plot were within reach.

CHAPTER 28

That feeling of optimism lasted until early afternoon the next day, when my phone chimed with Karen's special ringtone.

Without preamble, she dropped a bombshell. "My guys just got back to me with bad news. Paul's not a viable suspect."

"Shit!" I exclaimed. "What happened? You said yesterday that they liked him for it."

"They did," she confirmed. "What struck them initially was how much he hates Carolyn. They said it spews out even when he tries to control himself."

"We knew that already, although it's interesting that he couldn't contain himself even when he was being questioned by the police. Anything else?"

"Mm-hmm. Turns out that he collaborated on a case with one of the patent lawyers last year. The case involved a biotech startup that had a problem with patent rights on a drug they developed."

"That sounds good," I responded with interest. "Working on a case like that would have given Paul ample opportunity to learn about drug development."

"It gets even better. The major issue was that confidential material had been stolen during the review of an NIH grant."

"Aha! Exactly the kind of thing Carolyn was charged with, so Paul would have become familiar with NIH procedures."

"Right," Karen agreed. "And he also would have gotten to know people in the business who could have helped find Monica a job."

My enthusiasm was growing by leaps and bounds. "What's the problem then? Working the case would have given Paul the science background he needed, and the motive's there in spades. Sounds like he's a perfect fit."

"Except that he has an ironclad alibi for when Evans was murdered. He couldn't have set up the hit."

"Are you sure?" I asked. "All it would have taken is a phone call or two."

She didn't answer right away, which told me she thought it was a stupid question. As, in retrospect, it was. I was about to apologize, but she spoke first.

"Of course, I'm sure. Do you think I'd toss out our only suspect lightly?"

"I'm sorry, that was a stupid thing for me to say. It just popped out."

"You're right, it was stupid. But no harm done. Anyway, that's why the detectives didn't get back to me until a few minutes ago. They were trying to break his story but couldn't. Turns out he was on a fishing trip up north with two of his buddies from work. They spent three nights in an isolated lodge with no internet or cell service."

"And I take it there's plenty of confirmation for that?" I asked, albeit a little hesitantly.

"I'm afraid so. And not just from Paul's buddies. The reason this took so long is that my guys went up to the lodge and talked to the owner and his wife. They confirmed that Paul was there, and the only communication to the outside is by satellite phone. They have one, but Paul didn't use it."

"So Paul's in the clear," I acknowledged, getting my head around this new reality. "Unless maybe he was working with someone else who decided to take out Evans on their own."

"I suppose that's possible, and we'll keep on it," Karen said. "But

I'm not overly hopeful at this point. Do you think you can get any additional leads from Carolyn?"

"I don't think so. Maybe it's time to try a different approach."

"I hope you're saying that because you have something in mind. What are you thinking?"

"We know this all started because somebody got Monica to frame Carolyn. We've been looking at it from the standpoint of who had a motive to harm Carolyn. Instead, I'm going to try asking who was in a position to manipulate Monica. Maybe I can find something in Monica's background that'll help identify someone she was either indebted to or threatened by."

"I don't understand." Karen sounded puzzled. "What are you going to do, interview her family, friends, the usual kind of police stuff? I can have my detectives do that kind of thing, but I don't see how it connects to the case."

I smiled to myself. It wasn't often that Karen didn't get what I was thinking. Usually before I even thought it. "No, I'm not talking about that kind of stuff. I mean her scientific background, to see if I can find anyone who had the leverage to get her involved in this mess. Maybe that'll lead to someone who might benefit from Carolyn being accused of plagiarism."

"Oh, sorry! Now I see what you're after. And yes, that makes sense. Hope you have better luck with it than we've had so far."

She didn't sound terribly optimistic. Which was fair enough. I wasn't sure how optimistic I felt either. Reconstructing Monica's professional network from the dry record I had of her scientific career wouldn't be easy. And connecting that network to Carolyn in any meaningful way would be harder still.

But we didn't have much else going for us, so I figured I might as well give it a try.

CHAPTER 29

started by taking a fresh look at Monica's CV. She'd been an undergrad at UCLA and then gone to graduate school in biochemistry at Berkeley. Her thesis was on the nature of interactions between small molecules and proteins—an appropriate prelude to her current drug development work—and she'd published several papers in good journals with her graduate advisor. After completing her PhD, she stayed in San Francisco as a postdoctoral fellow at the UCSF School of Medicine where she'd worked on the identification of inhibitors of some of the protein kinases implicated in human cancer. She spent a productive five years in that capacity, again with good publications and a useful drug to show for her efforts.

That combination of success in both her graduate and postdoctoral work carried her on to a faculty position as an assistant professor at Westmark. Unfortunately, the six years that she'd been there, with her own lab, had been less productive. Her publications as an independent investigator were in no better than average journals. Nor did she have any significant discoveries to her credit.

It all fit my earlier assessment that she'd have had a hard time getting tenure. Except that she'd recently published a paper in *Cancer Treatment*, the most prestigious journal in the field. It had the reputation of publishing only the very best papers. Ones that were rigorously reviewed, not only to ensure that the science was flawless, but also on the basis of their impact and significance. For a young investigator like Monica, a paper in *Cancer Treatment* could make their career. And, as I recalled Carolyn telling me had happened for Monica, gain the support of their department in a tenure case.

There must have been a major breakthrough in Monica's research, and I was curious to see what had happened, so I went to the *Cancer Treatment* website and downloaded her paper. At first I read through it quickly, just to get the gist, but I couldn't see what the big deal was. It didn't look to me like the kind of major advance that *Cancer Treatment* normally published.

Figuring that I must be too preoccupied to get the point, I got a fresh cup of coffee, closed my office door, and forced myself to concentrate on reading the paper carefully. An hour later, I was even more puzzled. This just wasn't a *Cancer Treatment* paper. It reported that a minor modification of a drug used against breast cancer worked a bit better than the starting compound. But only a little better, not any kind of dramatic improvement. The results were worth publishing, but in one of the average quality journals Monica's other papers were in. Not in the most prestigious journal in the field.

As if that weren't enough, there was also a significant problem with a key experiment. Most of the experiments in the paper compared the activity of the starting drug with Monica's derivative against breast cancer cell lines grown in culture. In these comparisons, the derivative showed a modest, but significant, increase in activity. The final experiment compared the two drugs in treatment of actual tumors in mice: a critical step beyond the studies in cell culture. Again, the derivative displayed somewhat greater activity. But in this setting, the difference between the derivative and the starting compound wasn't significant by the standard statistical analysis.

The authors argued that the derivative's apparently greater activity was meaningful and hadn't met the cutoff for statistical significance simply because the number of mice was too small. They'd therefore tried an alternative statistical test that scored the results as just within the range for significance. Looking at the data, I could imagine that explanation was true. But if I were reviewing the paper, there's no way I would have recommended that it be published. Instead, the authors should have been required to repeat the experiment using enough mice to ensure that a result with clearcut statistical significance was obtained. Without that, there were no valid grounds for claiming that the derivative was better than the starting compound against real tumors in mice.

There was something wrong with the publication of this paper in *Cancer Treatment.* And something even more off with it having served to secure Monica's tenure. Thinking that I might have misunderstood what Carolyn told me concerning the tenure question, I printed out a copy and took it down to her office.

When I asked if she'd read it, she shrugged. "I took a look at it when it came out. It's not really my area so I didn't read it closely. I was just interested because of Monica."

"And what did you think? You've published several papers in *Cancer Treatment.* Did this look like the kind of paper you'd expect to see there?"

"Honestly, I have to say no. It seemed like an incremental improvement on an existing drug. Not the kind of novel and important result they try to publish."

"That was my reaction, too. And when I read it carefully, I also noticed a problem with the one experiment they did in mice. Take a look at this."

I showed her the relevant section of the paper and watched her eyes widen as she read it. "Holy shit! How could this get published without statistically significant results? At least using the normal method of analysis. I never would have let this get through if I were the reviewer. And my experience with *Cancer Treatment* is that the editors demand first-rate science as well as papers with high impact."

"Making it very hard to see how this wound up there," I said. "And didn't you also tell me that this paper basically saved Monica's tenure situation?"

"That's what she told me. Before this came out, she didn't think her chances were very good. But after it was published, her chair congratulated her and told her she didn't need to worry."

"Hard to imagine," I said. "Unless he never looked at the paper, and the name of the journal was enough. Oh well, it's all water under the bridge now. I was just surprised when I read it and wanted to get your take on it."

Except I didn't really think it was water under the bridge. There was something screwy about both the paper's publication and its importance in Monica's tenure case. Could there be something here that provided leverage for someone to manipulate her?

Maybe a trip to Boston would help sort it out.

CHAPTER 30

The chair of pharmacology, which had been Monica's department, was a man named Aaron Morris. A quick look online told me that he was sixty-four years old, ten years my senior, and worked on the mechanisms of tissue damage during a heart attack. He'd been department chair for the last seven years, and what was left of his lab was only marginally active, with a single paper published over a year ago being the most recent contribution. Probably a victim of the toll that administrative responsibilities can take on a chair's research.

If I were looking for someone in a position to exert pressure on Monica, he was a perfect candidate. She'd been worried about getting tenure, and as her department chair, Morris would have had a major say in that decision. I didn't see any basis for a connection between him and Carolyn, but he was certainly someone I needed to talk to.

I sent him a carefully worded email requesting a meeting, explaining that I was helping the Maine State Police with an investigation of Monica Kushman's murder by clarifying some of her scientific background. If he ignored me, I'd have Karen take the next and more official step.

But I was surprised by his prompt and friendly response.

I remember you from when you were here in Boston, before you went up north. And I'd be happy to talk to you about Monica. Would lunch on Thursday work?

A promising start. And given Westmark's location near Chinatown, meeting for lunch had special appeal. Really good Chinese food was one of the things I'd missed since moving to Maine.

———

The Thursday morning traffic was no worse than usual, and I managed to find a convenient parking place without difficulty, so I arrived ten minutes early. I thought about taking a walk to kill some time but decided that I might as well find his office and wait there until Morris was ready. To my surprise, there was no waiting. His assistant showed me in immediately, and a slightly overweight man with bushy white hair and sparkling blue eyes got up from behind his desk to greet me.

After brief introductions, he asked the question I'd been hoping for. "Do you like Chinese food? Dumplings, in particular."

I couldn't suppress a smile. "Absolutely. Dumplings are my favorite."

"There's a great place just a five-minute walk from here. Let's head out and beat the crowd."

We double-timed it down the street and got to the restaurant shortly before twelve. It was already getting crowded, but there were a few tables left, and we were seated promptly. Almost immediately, a waiter came over and poured tea.

"It's good to see you, Professor Morris. Would you like menus or should I bring you your usual?"

Morris looked at me with a faint smile of amusement. "I come here as often as I can. My usual is a combination of dumplings and steamed buns that Bo makes up for me. Together with some hot and sour soup. Or would you like to see a menu?"

"Your usual sounds good to me. I wouldn't want to mess with proven success."

He chuckled. "Two of the usual then, Bo. And go heavy on the dumplings. Any leftovers that we bring back to the office will have plenty of takers."

The soup arrived almost immediately, spicy and delicious. Bo returned with a platter of dumplings and steamed buns before we were finished and used a pair of chopsticks to point out the different offerings. The dumplings were filled with pork, chicken, and shrimp, some supplemented with Chinese cabbage or leeks. The fillings of the larger steamed buns included barbecued pork and my favorite, crispy duck with hoisin sauce.

We dug in happily for several minutes before I got around to asking about Monica. Morris didn't stop eating but slowed down enough to answer.

"She was among my first hires as chair, and I liked her from day one. She was one of those young scientists who always wanted to do the important experiment, the one that would change the field. She had good ideas, and she worked hard, but unfortunately things never quite panned out the way she hoped."

"Shooting too high can be a recipe for failure," I noted. "I hope she also had some safer projects that led to publications."

"Some. And I mentored her in that direction. But playing it safe wasn't what she wanted to do, and the bulk of her effort went into trying to tackle the really major questions. As a result, her productivity was marginal. I was afraid she'd wind up being denied tenure, but then she hit it big."

"You mean her paper in *Cancer Treatment*?"

"Mm-hmm. That was a home run in her field. And it gave her record the jolt it needed to get over the tenure bar."

I wondered if he knew how weak the paper really was. "Did you read it?" I asked.

He stopped with a pork and leek dumpling halfway to his mouth. "Of course I read it. And I take it from the question that you did too."

"I did," I acknowledged. "What'd you think of it?"

He frowned; the dumpling momentarily forgotten. "I guess it doesn't matter anymore. To be honest, I was surprised it got published in that journal. It's not my field, but it didn't seem particularly important, certainly not a big breakthrough. I don't believe Monica thought it was either. It was one of her safe projects, and I think she just submitted it there to see what would happen."

"That's what I thought, too. And I was really surprised when I saw some of the data weren't even statistically significant by the usual tests. I'd have rejected the paper if I'd been a reviewer."

"I know," he admitted. "I noticed that about the mouse experiments, too. The student who did that part of the work had already left Monica's lab for a job in industry, so I guess she just had to write up what he'd gotten done."

"That happens, although usually not with a paper in a top journal. But given the problems with the paper, aren't you surprised it got her tenure?"

He looked me in the eyes for a moment before answering. Then he shrugged. "I'm not sure why you're asking that. But like I said before, it doesn't matter anymore. You were a department chair, so you know how hard handling tenure cases can be. The career of a young faculty member is on the line, and you're in a position where you can pretty much make or break the case. Monica was a good scientist; she just didn't have good luck. But I liked her, and once that paper came out, I decided it made the record strong enough for me to support her. A few faculty in the department might have read the paper and recognized the problems, but we're a very diverse department, and most were just impressed by where the paper was published. And with my backing, a large majority voted in her favor. The case still had to be reviewed by a university-level committee, but nobody on that would have read the paper carefully enough to raise objections. Certainly not over my strong recommendation, and a nearly unanimous vote from the department."

I didn't doubt what he said. A strong chair could have a major influence, one way or the other, on a tenure case. Could he have used that influence to pressure Monica into sending Carolyn the grant when she was on study section? No doubt, but I didn't think he had. He was in a different field, and I couldn't imagine a reason for him to launch an attack on Carolyn.

Moreover, Aaron Morris wasn't someone who would have threatened or bribed Monica. He supported her because he liked her, and the paper in *Cancer Treatment* gave him the ammunition he needed to get her tenure.

But that left the question: How had the paper gotten published in *Cancer Treatment* in the first place?

Morris finally finished the dumpling and was about to pick up one of the steamed buns when I asked if he'd seen the reviewers' comments on the manuscript.

"No, I didn't need to. But all of Monica's things are still in her office, probably including her correspondence with the journal. You're welcome to have a look."

———

Two young women, I assumed students, were waiting in his outer office when we got back. Morris explained that he'd scheduled a meeting with them to listen to their complaints about the grading practices of one of his faculty members and asked his administrative assistant to take me to Monica's office. Then he handed her the few remaining dumplings we'd brought back, wished me luck, and turned his attention to his visitors with a show of much greater enthusiasm than I imagined he felt.

Monica's office appeared unchanged from my previous visit. There was a single four-drawer file cabinet, which I figured was the likely home of what I was after. The top drawer was labeled, "Manuscripts," so I started there. And right in front there was a file labeled, "Cancer Treatment Paper."

I took the file to the desk and sat down to go through it. There were some reprints of the published paper in front, followed by copies of the manuscript that appeared to represent the original submission and a revised version. And then there was the material I was after. Copies of Monica's correspondence with the journal.

I started with the journal's response to her original submission. As I would have expected, it informed her that the paper was not acceptable for publication in *Cancer Treatment*. The associate editor who'd handled the paper, a Leonard Frankel, said that it had been evaluated by three expert reviewers, all of whom questioned the significance of the work. They also had major concerns about the lack of statistical validity of the mouse data, as well as several minor points about other aspects of the experimental design. The editor hoped that the reviewers' criticisms would help her revise the manuscript for submission to another journal. He also noted that she was free to submit a revised manuscript addressing these criticisms to *Cancer Treatment* but cautioned that he would send it to the same reviewers, and given the nature of their criticisms, he could not predict a positive outcome.

I next looked at the reviewers' comments. Consistent with the associate editor's letter, they were unequivocally negative, and all three flatly recommended that the paper be rejected.

Most people would have taken that for a firm rejection and sent the paper to a less demanding journal. But Monica had instead decided to try resubmitting a revised manuscript. Her cover letter argued that the reviewers had missed the point, and the results actually represented a major advance in the methodology used for drug synthesis. An argument that I thought was bullshit and had zero chance of success. And her response to the problem all three reviewers had raised with the lack of statistical validity of the mouse data was to add the nonstandard analysis I'd been surprised to see in the published paper.

There was no way I could imagine the reviewers reacting favorably, so I looked next to see their comments on this revised manuscript. But there weren't any. Instead, there was only a brief form letter from the journal's managing editor.

Dear Dr. Kushman,

I am pleased to inform you that your revised manuscript is now acceptable for publication in Cancer Treatment. *Thank you for giving us the opportunity to publish your outstanding work.*

Margaret Pollard, Managing Editor

I had to read it twice. It made no sense, none at all. The associate editor who'd handled the original manuscript had flatly rejected it, and this revision wasn't improved in any significant way. But he'd apparently changed his mind and accepted it, without even sending it back to the reviewers.

Could the letter of acceptance have been sent in error? I'd never heard of a mistake like that, but anything was possible.

Otherwise, something really bizarre was going on.

CHAPTER 31

The editorial offices of *Cancer Treatment* were in Kendall Square, an area adjacent to MIT that had become a major center of biotechnology. It was more or less on my way home, so I figured I might as well make a stop there before driving back to Maine. I wasn't sure how much I'd learn, but it couldn't hurt to try talking to the associate editor who'd handled Monica's manuscript. Maybe I'd get lucky.

But that approach never got off the ground. When I asked for Leonard Frankel at the reception desk, I was told that he no longer worked at *Cancer Treatment*. And no, the receptionist had no idea how I might contact him.

My only other option was to ask to speak to Margaret Pollard, the managing editor. The receptionist first said that Ms. Pollard didn't normally take meetings without an appointment, but when I told her that I was visiting from Maine where I was director of the Maine Translational Research Institute, she relented and said she'd check. After a quick phone call, she smiled brightly and led me down a hall to the managing editor's office.

The office was small and cluttered with stacks of manuscripts and correspondence. Pretty much what I'd expect for a managing editor.

Margaret Pollard, however, was not. She was young, not over thirty, with long black hair and bright, intelligent eyes that moved rapidly, as if she didn't want to miss anything happening around her.

After inviting me to sit in a visitor chair across from her desk, which required clearing away a pile of papers, she asked what she could do for me. Pleasant, but efficient and to the point.

I explained that I was assisting the Maine State Police with the investigation of Monica Kushman's murder and was interested in the background of a paper she'd recently published in *Cancer Treatment*. I'd hoped to talk to Leonard Frankel about it, but understood he was no longer here.

"That's correct," she confirmed. "He left unexpectedly a few weeks ago. It's been even crazier than usual around here, with the two other associate editors trying to do his work as well as their own."

"I can imagine. Do you have his contact information? I'd very much like to speak with him."

"I'm afraid not. His departure was weird." She looked amused. "Said he'd had enough of the daily grind and was going to take off on a cross-country motorcycle trip while he figured out what he wanted to do in life. Sort of like a nineteen-sixties hippie."

"Huh! That's weird all right. Somehow not what I'd expect from a journal editor, but I guess you never know. He didn't leave a phone number or anything?" I asked.

"No. I have his old cell phone number, but I tried, and it's no longer in service. Is there something I can do to help?"

"I hope so. He was the associate editor who handled the paper of Kushman's that I'm interested in. Its trajectory at the journal was somewhat odd, and I was hoping he could tell me more about it. Anything you can tell me in his absence would be great."

I showed her the original and revised manuscripts, the reviewers' comments, and the editorial correspondence I'd taken from Kushman's office. In her position as managing editor—not a scientific editor—I wasn't sure she'd understand what bothered me. But maybe she'd remember something helpful.

When I finished, however, she surprised me. "You probably know that my job is just to oversee the process of review and publication, not to evaluate the science. But I see what you mean about this being odd. And it's not at all consistent with the way we normally handle the review process." She frowned in puzzlement. "I really don't get it. We keep track of the flow of manuscripts electronically; let me see what I can find in the database."

She spent several minutes on her computer before looking up. Her expression was even more perplexed. "The manuscript started out through the review process normally. I logged it in when it was received and assigned it to Frankel as associate editor. He found three reviewers, and I sent them the manuscript. The reviews came back promptly, and I noted on my spreadsheet that all three recommended rejecting the manuscript without encouraging resubmission. Frankel took it to the executive meeting the next week—"

I interrupted her mid-sentence. "What's that? Sorry to interrupt."

"That's okay. All three associate editors meet weekly with the editor-in-chief, Dr. Horrigan, to discuss those manuscripts whose reviews have come in. The one handling the manuscript gives the group a summary and presents the reviewers' recommendations. The group—really Dr. Horrigan—then decides on disposition of the paper. Either accept, accept with modification, or reject. Which can be either with or without encouraging resubmission."

"I'm surprised that Horrigan has the time for weekly meetings like that," I commented. "You probably don't realize how famous he is, but he's an incredibly busy man."

"Oh, I'm well aware. He's a chaired professor at Harvard, director of a major center for innovative chemistry with a large lab of his own, and a featured speaker at God knows how many conferences each year. Not to mention traveling frequently to Washington for all sorts of government committee meetings. But the journal is a pet project, and he sees it as his responsibility to participate in those weekly meetings so he can make sure that we publish only top-quality manuscripts. When he's away, we set them up on Zoom."

"Sounds like you know him pretty well; I'm surprised you have all that at your fingertips."

She smiled. "He's an impressive man but also a nice guy. Always stops in to say hi and ask me how school's going when he's here."

I was curious about that. "School?" I asked.

"Being a managing editor's just a temporary job to help me pay tuition while I'm in law school," she explained. "This is my last year. But should we get back to Kushman's paper?"

"Sure, I didn't mean to distract you."

"No problem. Anyway, Frankel presented it at the meeting and the decision was to reject without encouraging resubmission. He then sent her the letter you showed me earlier."

"But she chose to resubmit anyway," I remarked.

"As was her right, although that's generally just a waste of time. With a resubmitted manuscript, the associate editor usually has it re-reviewed, although he can also make a final decision on his own at that point. If the manuscript was initially rejected, I would have expected him either to send it back to the reviewers or to reject it outright. Given the flimsiness of her rebuttal, I'd have thought it would have been outright rejection."

"But instead, he accepted it?"

She spread her hands in a gesture of puzzlement. "I just checked my records. He emailed me the usual note saying to accept, and I then sent Kushman our standard acceptance letter. I remember being surprised to see it accepted after initially getting a firm rejection, but sometimes an author can make major improvements, and that happens."

"But that wasn't the case this time," I said.

"No, it certainly wasn't," she agreed. "Now that you've shown me the manuscripts, I don't see how Frankel could have recommended acceptance. It makes me wonder if he wanted to reject it and sent me the wrong email by mistake."

CHAPTER 32

texted Karen as soon as I got back to my car. The story was too complicated to put in a short message, but I wanted to share my excitement at having finally made some progress.

This was a good trip! I'll fill you in tonight, too much to go through now. But bottom line is that an associate editor accepted Monica's paper after it had been rejected by reviewers and the other editors. Not supposed to happen that way, and it smells like a bribe to make her set up Carolyn. The guy has since left the journal, and we'll have to find him, but at least we know who we're looking for.

I'd expected a quick response, either by text or phone. But it was over an hour later when I finally heard from her.

That's great! Sorry it took me so long to get back. It's crazy here with a robbery and shooting in Biddeford. Afraid I'll be late tonight. Not sure when, you may have to tell me about it in the morning.

Disappointing. Not just because I'd miss having her home but also because I'd been looking forward to getting her perspective on the day's events. But this would give me tonight to do some background work on Leonard Frankel.

The simplest possibility was that Frankel was the head honcho—the driving force behind the plot to get Carolyn. But it was also possible that he'd been used by someone else as a tool to manipulate Monica. To fully sort that out, we'd have to get our hands on him and make him talk. Which meant finding him on his cross-country motorcycle trip, if that was indeed what he was doing. But Karen could enlist the aid of the FBI, and finding people was something they were good at. In the meantime, I thought I'd do a little research and see if he'd had any interactions with Carolyn that could have spurred a desire for revenge.

But first things first. Rosie was waiting impatiently at the door when I got home, so I cuddled her, fed her, and took her for a walk on the beach. She got rid of some of her pent-up energy by chasing seagulls and playing with the waves, while I called Carolyn to ask if she knew Leonard Frankel. I didn't add that he'd been an associate editor of *Cancer Treatment* because I wanted to see what she came up with on her own.

"The name rings a vague bell, but I can't think from where. Maybe I met him at a conference or something like that. Let me search my email and see if anything comes up."

I thought that meeting him at a conference had some promise. Maybe they'd had some kind of disagreement that she forgot about while he stayed angry. Or maybe he made a pass at her, and she shot him down.

But I was disappointed when she came back on the line. "No, it wasn't a conference. He was the associate editor who handled one of my papers at *Cancer Treatment* a couple of years ago."

"Ah, I guess I should have told you he'd been with *Cancer Treatment*. Did you interact with him at all?"

"Just routine editorial correspondence. The reviewers liked the paper, and it was accepted after minor revision. Nothing beyond that, and I'm pretty sure I didn't even talk to him."

So no direct interaction with Carolyn. That left me with the alternative of digging into Frankel's background. I wasn't hungry after having gorged myself on Chinese dumplings for lunch, so I decided to skip dinner and just take out a couple slices of leftover frozen pizza in case I wanted something later. I took some out for Karen too while I was at it, in case she was hungry when she got home. Then I poured a glass of scotch and went upstairs with Rosie to hit the computer.

I started with the *Cancer Treatment* website, which had brief bios of the associate editors. Fortunately, Frankel's was still there. He'd obtained his PhD in microbiology and immunology from the University of Kentucky in 2017. He'd then been a postdoctoral researcher at the University of Texas for four years before joining the *Cancer Treatment* editorial staff in 2021. As a personal note, the bio added that he lived in Cambridge with his cat and was an avid motorcyclist.

It was the kind of career progression that wasn't uncommon for young scientists who found that they didn't want to pursue research, either in academia or industry, and therefore made an alternative career choice. A full-time teaching position was one possibility, but a career as a science writer or editor was another option that allowed them to put their training to good use.

It seemed like that had been Frankel's situation, but I decided to go a step further and check out his publication record using PubMed, the National Library of Medicine's database of scientific publications. He'd published two papers as a graduate student, both dealing with the immune response to tumors in mice. He'd then done postdoctoral work in a lab that was working on one of the cancer immunotherapies that had shown striking success in recent years. It was an exciting area and a good choice of direction for Frankel to have made. While he apparently hadn't wanted a research career himself, his training in immunotherapy would have given him valuable contacts and a perspective that fit with the range of papers published in *Cancer Treatment*.

But there was nothing in his background that was related to Carolyn's work in drug development, and I figured he had to be at least ten years younger than she was. In the absence of any connection between them, I had to suspect that Frankel wasn't the mastermind behind the plot but had been used by a third party to secure Monica's involvement.

I shut down the computer just as Rosie announced Karen's arrival by jumping up and racing downstairs to the front door, barking at the top of her lungs. I followed a bit behind her, and Karen greeted us both with hugs and kisses, the kisses being rather more intimate for me than for Rosie.

When we took a break, Karen asked the question I figured would be at the top of her list. "Do we have anything to eat? I'm starved."

I smiled. "I didn't have dinner either, but I took out some of the leftover pizza to thaw. A couple slices for me and a couple for you. Should I go heat them up?"

"Please! How come you haven't had dinner?"

"I had an enormous lunch of Chinese dumplings with the guy who was chair of Monica's department. But I'll tell you about that and the rest of my day shortly." We went into the kitchen, and I put the pizza in the oven. "This should just take a few minutes. What's been going on with you?"

"It was a pile of crap. Two guys with guns held up a convenience store. The owner tried to resist and one of the perps shot him."

"Jesus, is he. . . ."

Karen shook her head in response to my unfinished question. "No, thank God. He was hit in the shoulder and will be okay. Meantime, the perps grabbed a few hundred in cash and got away."

"Any leads?"

"The owner was able to identify one who had two priors. Long story short, they were eventually picked up in Kittery." She shook her head sadly. "Two kids really, eighteen and nineteen years old."

"And now they're facing long jail terms for a couple of hundred bucks. So damn stupid."

Karen sighed. "That describes a lot of what I deal with. But on a more cheerful note, I can smell the pizza. Think it's ready?"

I took it out of the oven while Karen got plates down from the cabinet. At first, I gave us two slices each, but then thought better of it and transferred one of mine to Karen's plate.

She grinned. "Good man! I take it you're not about to starve?"

"Don't worry, I can still almost taste the dumplings from lunch."

We took our plates to the table, and Karen took a first bite. "Delicious. Okay, tell me about your day while we eat."

She listened attentively while I recounted my meetings with Monica's department chair and the *Cancer Treatment* managing editor, followed by what I'd learned about Leonard Frankel online. The pizza was gone by the time I finished.

"That sounds a helluva lot more interesting than my day was." There was a note of excitement in her voice. "Let me see if I have this all straight. Your dumpling buddy agreed with you that Monica's paper was lousy but was happy to use it to get her tenure anyway. Then you found her correspondence with the journal, and it turned out the reviewers thought her paper was lousy too. The editor, this Leonard Frankel, initially rejected it but then turned around and accepted a resubmitted manuscript that hadn't been much improved."

"Which the managing editor said was counter to the journal's normal operating policy," I added.

"Understood. So you think he pulled a fast one in order to gain leverage over Monica. And now he's in the wind, having left his job and taken off on some whacky motorcycle trip."

"That sums it up. Seems to me it would be far too coincidental for him not to be involved."

"Oh, I agree. But you don't think he's the man in charge?"

"I don't. He's a lot younger than Carolyn, they've been at different universities, and their research areas are distinct. She doesn't think they ever met, and there's nothing to suggest he had any motive for going after her."

"What do you think happened then?" she asked.

"I'm betting the head honcho either blackmailed or bribed Frankel. There's no way to know if he was a candidate for blackmail, but he apparently lives alone, and I can imagine a juicy enough bribe could entice him to pull up roots and make a fresh start somewhere else."

"Okay, I can see that. In any case, the thing we have to do is find him and get him to talk. Do you think he's really on a cross-country motorcycle trip?"

I shrugged. "Good question. His bio on the journal website does say he's a motorcycle enthusiast. But who knows? That could have just been a cover."

"Doesn't really matter. I'll start a nationwide search tomorrow morning, and we'll find him." She got up and came over to give me a kiss. "I do believe you're making progress, Professor."

CHAPTER 33

Karen expected it would take at least several days to track down Frankel, so I was surprised to get a call from her just two days later.

"The Massachusetts State Police found him. No motorcycle trip, he was just hanging out at a cabin in the Berkshires."

"That's great! Are they bringing him up here or should we go down there to talk to him?"

She sighed. "I'm afraid there isn't going to be any talking to him. He's dead. Shot in what they thought was a home invasion gone bad."

"Shit! I can't believe it. You don't think it was really a botched robbery, do you? This is the second witness who could have identified the head honcho but turns up dead before we can question them."

"No, too much coincidence for it to have been a burglary. Now that I've talked to them, our friends in Massachusetts don't think so either. They're working the case from their end."

"And? Have they turned up anything?" I asked hopefully.

"Not much, but it's early days, and the crime scene guys are still going over everything. The house was pretty thoroughly ransacked, either to make it look like a burglary or because the killers were after something. But there is one interesting thing. Frankel recently bought a house on Martha's Vineyard. Paid over a million and a half in cash, which didn't come out of any bank account the investigators could find."

I tried to think of an innocent explanation. "Maybe from his family? Or an inheritance?"

"No, they already checked the obvious sources. I think you were right about him having been bribed to set up Monica."

"And then he was killed when the boss learned I was asking questions about what happened with the paper." That made Frankel the third person who'd been murdered because of my inquiries. Not a thought I was thrilled with, although Evans didn't merit any tears.

"It looks like it. Raising the question of who knew you were digging into how the paper was handled. Monica's old department chair and people at the journal office?"

"The department chair knew I wanted to look at her correspondence with the journal, but he had a meeting and had his assistant take me to Monica's office. I didn't see him afterward, so he wouldn't have known I found anything noteworthy."

"Unless he's the one we're after, and he already knew what you were going to find," Karen pointed out.

It was an interesting thought. I took a moment to consider it, but it didn't play right.

"I don't think so," I finally replied. "If he knew the correspondence was incriminating, he'd have destroyed it rather than leaving it in her office for me or someone else to find."

"Good point," she acknowledged. "And you were pretty convinced from meeting him anyway, so let's take him off the list. Who did you talk to at the journal offices?"

"Just the receptionist and the managing editor. I didn't say much to the receptionist, although I did initially ask to talk to Frankel. And I don't think the managing editor's a candidate. She's just doing this to help pay her tuition for law school. But I'll give her a call and see if she told anyone else about my visit. Maybe she talked to the wrong person."

————

I was surprised when Margaret Pollard sounded pleased to hear from me. When I said so, she laughed. "Well, what can I say? You were easy to talk to the other day, and you didn't cause any major hassles for me. Which is different from most of the visitors a managing editor gets. What can I do for you?"

"Just a follow-up question. But first, I'm afraid I have some bad news. Leonard Frankel's been murdered."

I could feel her shock through the phone line. "Murdered! That's terrible. What happened?"

"The police think it was a home invasion gone awry."

"That's so sad, just when he was on his big cross-country motor-cycle adventure. We weren't close or anything, but it's a shock to have that happen to someone you know. I'm surprised he was even in a home, rather than camping by the roadside or something."

"It doesn't seem that he was actually on a trip. The Massachusetts State Police found him at a cabin in the Berkshires."

There was a pause on the line. "I see. How odd. Is that why you called me? You're not thinking this could somehow be related to the paper we talked about, are you?"

She was quick. But I wasn't ready to share my suspicions with her. "Oh, I think that's pretty unlikely. But I did want to see who you might have talked to about my visit."

"Uh-huh. And you probably have a nice bridge in Brooklyn you'd like to sell me. Oh well, maybe I'll find out what's going on someday. Anyway, I told Dr. Horrigan when I saw him the next day. I thought he should know what had happened in case he wanted to publish some kind of correction. And I was worried he might be angry that we'd made a mistake, so I wanted to be the one who told him about it."

"How'd he react?" I asked.

"He was shocked but really nice about it. Said it wasn't my fault, and there wasn't any need for the journal to publish an apology or anything. No harm had been done, since nothing was wrong with the paper that would mislead other scientists, not as if it was fraud. It just wasn't up to our normal standards."

"That makes sense. I'm glad he didn't blame you for it."

"Not at all. He just said it was nice that Frankel had quit so he didn't have to bother firing him. Then he held a meeting with me and the two remaining associate editors to come up with a new safety check procedure so mistakes like this don't happen again. Basically, I'm now supposed to verify that a decision letter is consistent with the last round of reviews. If it's not, I get back to the associate editor for confirmation before sending it out."

"I guess that's a bit more work for you, but it makes sense. So the two associate editors are the only ones at the journal who know what happened?" I asked. "Besides Dr. Horrigan and yourself, I mean."

"As far as I know. Jason White and Marvin Dent. I suppose one of them could have said something to his assistant, but that doesn't seem likely."

I thanked her and ended the call, thinking it might have been useful. I was confident that she wasn't the culprit, and Emil Horrigan was above suspicion. But the two associate editors were potential suspects.

I'd have to ask Carolyn if she knew either of them, but today was the day I was scheduled to attend the board of trustees meeting to present my proposal for her retention. That gave me just over half an hour, so I decided to put off talking to Carolyn and see what I could find online about White and Dent instead.

Their biographical paragraphs on the journal website indicated that they had received their PhDs in 2016 from the University of Florida and 2017 from the University of Rhode Island, respectively. They'd both done postdocs of a few years and then assumed their present positions.

Those career trajectories were very similar to Leonard Frankel's, which I confirmed by checking their publication records. That seemed to be the type Horrigan liked to hire as associate editors—young people who didn't want to pursue a career in research but who were knowledgeable enough about their areas to adjudicate the fate of manuscripts submitted to the journal. Under Horrigan's watchful eye, of course.

Also, like Frankel, there wasn't anything in either of their records that suggested any sort of overlap with Carolyn. White's field was radiation therapy, unrelated to Carolyn's work. Dent's research had focused on chemotherapy but using approaches that were different from the kind of work Carolyn did.

One of them could still have crossed paths with her at some point, and it was worth running their names by her. But I wasn't optimistic and had to admit that I'd probably hit another dead end. Maybe we'd get lucky, and the cops investigating Frankel's murder would turn up something.

I thought of calling Karen to tell her the news, but it was time for me to switch gears and go to the trustees' meeting. I gathered up the summary of Carolyn's accomplishments I'd put together for the occasion: the number of papers she'd published, how many patents she held, and—no doubt most important for the trustees—the amount of grant funding she'd brought into the institute over the years. Also, because James Cameron had suggested it might be an issue, notes on the discussions I'd had with her in which she'd agreed to accept the retention package I was proposing.

Then I told Anna I'd be back in a couple of hours and went out to my car.

CHAPTER 34

he trustees' meetings were held at the Cliff House, a well-known luxury hotel perched above the ocean on Bald Head Cliff in Ogunquit. It was only about a half hour from MTRI, but I felt like I'd entered a different world when I drove up a long cobblestone driveway through carefully landscaped grounds to a complex of gleaming gray-and-white buildings. A uniformed attendant took my car, and I went in to ask for directions to the MTRI trustees' meeting at the front desk, after which I was escorted to one of the hotel's private dining rooms.

The room where the meeting was held featured a glass-paneled wall and a sliding door leading out to a terrace with a panoramic view of the ocean. Most of the trustees were already milling about on the terrace with glasses of wine and watching the waves crash into the rocky shore below. The chairman, James Cameron, greeted me and said he was just waiting for two more trustees to arrive before starting the meeting. Once everyone was seated and lunch was served, he was planning to raise Carolyn's case as the first order of business and call on me for the presentation. He thought everything would go smoothly, although he'd heard rumblings of resistance from one or two of the board members.

Before I could ask what sort of rumblings he was talking about, we were interrupted by the arrival of the remaining trustees, and Cameron asked everyone to come inside so we could get started. Four round tables, each with a half-dozen place settings, were arranged around a podium in the front of the room. Our places were marked with name cards, and I was pleased to find myself sitting next to Isabelle Fisher. At least I'd have a friend close by.

Lunch was served as soon as we were all seated. It looked good. Lobster tails were accompanied by parmesan truffle fries and a spinach salad with goat cheese and candied walnuts. Karen would have loved it, but in her absence, I'd have to enjoy it on my own.

Unfortunately, Cameron called the meeting to order just as I was taking my first bite. I hoped they'd do something like discuss the minutes of the last meeting, but no. He simply said that this afternoon's principal item of business was the proposed retention of Dr. Carolyn Gelman and asked me to present the case.

I rose to go to the podium as Isabelle whispered, "Good luck. I'll guard your lobster." Reassured that lunch wasn't lost, I thanked the trustees for all the support they'd given the institute over the years we'd worked together. As I hoped, that got me smiles and nods from the audience as I started to talk about Carolyn. First, I summarized her accomplishments and her value to MTRI, including her consistent record of sizable grant support from NIH. Then I reviewed the offer she'd received from Yale, noting that it reflected the high regard in which she was held by the rest of the scientific community. And finally, I discussed the retention package I'd worked out, reminding them that I'd take care of the equipment and operating funds from the institute's existing budget, but would need their help to establish an endowed chair with an appropriate salary increase.

When I finished, I thanked them for their attention and asked if there were any questions. The first hand to be raised was Isabelle's, who started off by praising my efforts in retaining such a valuable faculty member. She then lent her enthusiastic support to the proposal, saying that Carolyn more than deserved the additional salary and recognition that an endowed chair would bring. Her comments were greeted with obvious approval from the group, and I figured we were in good shape.

Two other trustees had questions about the impact of Carolyn's grant funding on the institute's overall budget, and I took the opportunity to explain how we received indirect costs in addition to direct costs from NIH grants. While the direct costs went specifically to the grantee's research, the indirect costs were used for general institutional needs, including common facilities and shared equipment. As a result, each investigator's grants contributed to the general funding pool, as well as supporting their individual research project. The trustees got it, with one commenting that he liked the way I could use Carolyn's grant funding to offset other expenses, noting that it made her retention a sound investment in the institute's future. All I could do was smile and thank him.

It looked like we were done, and Cameron was about to call for a vote when one of the trustees sitting at a table next to Isabelle raised his hand. I recognized him as Marvin Hemming, a neurosurgeon at a prestigious Harvard-affiliated hospital. He was a member of an old-money Boston family with, among several other properties, an ocean-front estate in Wells that served as his summer home. I didn't know him well but assumed he was on the board both because of his connections to the Boston medical establishment and his deep pockets.

When I called on him, Hemming glowered at me and addressed the room with a voice laden with sarcasm. "This mutual admiration is all very nice, but I can't believe you people are ready to approve this deal. Am I the only one who's bothered by the obvious problem with it all?"

So, here's the resistance Cameron started to tell me about. "What problem are you referring to?" I asked. Politely, I hoped.

"I'm talking about why the hell would she turn down a high-level job at a top university like Yale to stay at a backwater place like MTRI. Your retention isn't even offering her more than they are; just meeting their terms."

Patience, I told myself. "Well, as I explained earlier, she likes it here and that's more important to her than Yale's prestige. Plus, she's not interested in taking on the administrative duties of a center director at this stage of her career."

"That's bullshit. Yale's offering her the kind of job most people would kill for. Nobody I know would turn it down to stay here. Only reason I can imagine is that she's afraid she won't make it at a top-notch place, that she's not good enough to play with the big boys. And if that's the case, there's no reason for us to offer a fancy counter."

I was fighting hard to control my temper. But it was a losing battle, and I was about to give up. It might not be smart, but the urge to lay into this jerk was overpowering.

But Isabelle went for him first. In a voice loud enough to carry to the front of the room, she muttered, "Fucking sexist pig."

Hemming turned red. "What the hell did you say?!"

"I called you a fucking sexist pig. There's no way you'd say crap like that about a man. Not good enough to play with the big boys, my ass. If it was a man, you'd be falling all over yourself to keep him."

It looked like he started to say something, but it was drowned out by applause and exclamations of "Hear, hear!" from most of the women and many of the men in the room. Together with mocking laughter and a few catcalls of "Oink, oink."

Poor Hemming—yes, I'd started to think of him that way—sat back looking shocked. Then he muttered something under his breath and stomped out as Cameron pounded his water glass with a knife in an effort to restore order. When the room finally quieted, Isabelle raised her hand and moved for approval of my proposed counteroffer. There were several seconds, and Cameron asked for a voice vote, which was loud and unanimous.

I returned to my seat, happy with the outcome and ready to finally have lunch. Except my lobster was gone. Isabelle must have been too distracted to protect it from an overzealous waiter. When she saw what had happened, she started to apologize, but I assured her that watching her skewer Hemming had been worth the sacrifice.

CHAPTER 35

I was looking forward to getting back to MTRI and sharing the good news with Carolyn. Now that the trustees had approved my proposal, I could present her with an official letter spelling out the details of the offer. I already had the letter drafted in my head, so it wouldn't take long to have Anna put in on paper. Two copies, with a place for Carolyn to sign at the bottom.

The drive back to MTRI was slow-going, especially around Ogunquit's town center, even though the summer tourist traffic was a thing of the past. Once I had Carolyn's letter laid out, I let my mind wander back to Isabelle's takedown of Hemming. She'd hit the nail on the head. He was an arrogant, sexist jackass. But he'd said something that stuck in my head.

Yale is offering her the kind of job most people would kill for.

He hadn't meant it literally, of course. People say things like that all the time. *My mom'll kill me if I get less than a B in math.*

But could an alternative candidate have wanted the job at Yale badly enough to play dirty by trying to discredit Carolyn? The sad fact was that it wasn't unusual for scientists to slander a competitor. I'd never heard of anything as complicated as the plagiarism accusations, but it wasn't beyond the realm of imagination. Murder might be unthinkable, but that had come later when Monica was on the verge of exposing everything. At that point, perhaps fear of discovery had driven the perpetrator to desperation.

It seemed crazy, but by the time I made it back to MTRI, I decided it wouldn't hurt to see who the other candidates for the job at Yale had been. If Carolyn didn't know, I could always call Martin Dawson. It would at least give me a fresh window on potential suspects, with a list of names I could check to see if any of them had been in a position to manipulate Monica.

First, though, I had Anna prepare Carolyn's formal retention letter. After I signed for the institute, Anna asked if she should hand deliver it. I don't think she was surprised when I told her that I wanted the pleasure of doing that myself.

Not unexpectedly, Carolyn jumped out of her chair with excitement when I presented it to her. We spent several minutes congratulating each other over the happy outcome, while Molly kept darting her head back and forth between us trying to figure out what all the excitement was about. When Carolyn finally gave her a hug and told her it meant they could stay here in Maine, she wagged her tail and went back to sleep. That got another big smile from Carolyn as she signed off her agreement.

I took advantage of the interruption to change the topic and ask Carolyn if she knew either of the other two associate editors at *Cancer Treatment*, Jason White and Marvin Dent.

"Jason White was the editor on another paper of ours," she recalled. "It was uneventful, and I never spoke with him or anything. I haven't dealt with the other one you mentioned."

"And you didn't meet either of them at a conference or anything like that?"

She shook her head. "Why? Are you thinking they might have been involved in the plagiarism accusations?"

"It doesn't seem likely, but they did come up in discussion about it. Another question though. Who were the other candidates for the job at Yale?"

Her eyes widened. "You're not thinking it was one of them? I can't believe that, the search committee told me the other candidates were all eminent scientists. I don't know who they were though, that was kept confidential."

I stopped into my lab for half an hour or so after leaving Carolyn, just to check in and see how my students were doing. When I got back to my office, I called the dean's office at Yale and asked to be connected to Dean Dawson.

"You son of a bitch," was the first thing he said when he took my call.

I laughed. "Guess you've already heard from Carolyn."

"Stop smirking! Yeah, I just got an email from her. I can't believe you pulled this off."

"It wasn't easy. You guys obviously made her quite an offer. But the bottom line was that she's happy here."

"And that usually wins out in the end," he sighed. "Yeah, I know. Oh well, you win some and you lose some. At least I get to have dinner with you and Karen. Although I'm sure you'll make our little wager cost me a pretty penny."

"You can count on it. I have the restaurant all picked out. But first, I've got a question for you. Who were the other candidates for the position?"

"Sorry, we promised to keep that confidential. Why do you want to know?"

"It's too long a story to go through over the phone. I'll fill you in when we get together, but it's part of trying to figure out who brought the plagiarism charges against her."

"That's still going on?"

"It's actually grown considerably. There've been three murders in connection with covering it up."

"Holy shit! I knew about the first one, of course, but two more? And you guys think one of our alternate candidates could be behind it?"

Not surprisingly, he sounded shocked. "Just a possibility. We're stuck and looking under whatever rocks we can find," I explained.

"Got it. Well, there was actually only one other candidate who was seriously considered. He made us swear to confidentiality so that his home institution wouldn't find out, but there's no way he'd be behind anything crooked. If I told you who it was, you'd be embarrassed for asking."

"C'mon, Martin. I promise his name won't go any further, except for Karen. And I'll let you off the hook for dessert."

He chuckled. "You drive a hard bargain. All right, fine. It'll be public soon anyway, because we'll be offering him the job. Believe it or not, it's Emil Horrigan."

CHAPTER 36

mil Horrigan. The superstar I'd considered above suspicion. But I couldn't ignore the fact that his name had now come up twice. In his role as editor-in-chief of *Cancer Treatment,* he could have been responsible for publishing Monica's paper in return for her sending Carolyn the grant. He'd presumably offered Leonard Frankel, the associate editor, a hefty sum to accept the paper and then disappear.

But did I really think he'd had Monica killed? Followed by George Evans, and then by Leonard Frankel? Three murders, and for what? He already held an endowed chair and was director of a thriving center for innovative chemistry at Harvard. The job at Yale wasn't much different, so why would he want to move so desperately?

I didn't know the answer to that, but he was in the perfect position to manipulate Monica. And now there was a possible motive. He had to be considered a prime suspect.

I sat back and decided to reconstruct how he might have gone about setting things up. Identifying Carolyn as his competition would have been easy enough. Keeping search committee information confidential was more of a concept than a reality, and someone with Horrigan's stature and influence would have had no problem finding a friendly committee member who was overly forthcoming.

Choosing Monica for her role would also have been straightforward. She had probably come to his attention when her initial submission to *Cancer Treatment* was rejected. Or he may simply have checked the websites of Boston institutions to find potentially vulnerable junior faculty who worked in the area of drug development. When he examined Monica's CV, he'd have concluded—as I had—that she would have a hard time getting tenure. Making her susceptible to bribery with an offer to accept her paper and help her find a new position, if that were still necessary once she had a publication in *Cancer Treatment* to her credit.

He would also have needed information on submitted grants, so I checked the membership rosters of NIH advisory committees that I'd printed out to show Carolyn earlier. And there he was, chair of the National Cancer Institute Advisory Board, which would have given him access to summaries of pending applications. He wouldn't even have had to target Jackson's grant in particular. He just needed to identify an application that was similar enough to Carolyn's work to allow him to manufacture a plausible accusation of plagiarism. Easy enough, since there were always several such applications pending.

There was still one missing link though. It only made sense for Horrigan to have targeted Monica if he knew she was going to be on a study section that reviewed relevant grants. But the same weak record that made her susceptible to manipulation would have made her unlikely to be chosen by NIH, which normally selected reviewers with significant research accomplishments of their own. Making me wonder if he'd also engineered Monica's invitation to serve as a reviewer.

Monica had been on the Clinical Therapeutics study section, which was the group that reviewed most drug development grants. I'd served on that study section myself and knew the NIH administrator in charge, Carla Johansen. Simple enough to give her a call and see if she remembered how she'd decided to invite Monica as a reviewer.

Carla seemed pleased to hear from me when she answered the phone, probably because most of her calls came from applicants who were angry that their grant hadn't received a high enough rating to be funded. It was a tough business.

We exchanged pleasantries, and she asked why I was calling. "I'm betting it's not because you want to come and review grants for us again," she joked.

"I'm afraid you're right; being an institute director is keeping me a little too busy," I responded lightly. "There is something I'm hoping you can help me with in that regard, though. Do you remember Monica Kushman?"

"How could I forget that one? What a damn troublemaker, sending a confidential application to a friend. One of your colleagues at MTRI, right?"

"Yes, it was Carolyn Gelman. Which is why I'm interested. Do you remember how you chose Monica as a reviewer?"

"She had a paper coming out in *Cancer Treatment*," Carla responded quickly. "You know what an accomplishment it is to get something published there."

"Of course. But was it just the paper? I know you like to get references from people in the field."

This time there was a pause before she answered. "You're right, I do. And I got a very strong one for her."

"That's what I figured. From whom?"

"You know I can't tell you that. Those recommendations are highly confidential."

I took a deep breath and plunged ahead. "Carla, I'm asking in regard to a murder case I'm working on as a consultant to the Maine State Police. Monica Kushman's murder as a matter of fact. I can get a subpoena if necessary."

She paused again. "All right, I suppose it doesn't matter now. Emil Horrigan called me personally to say that I had to get her on study section. He was publishing a blockbuster paper that was going to put her on top of the field. It wasn't out yet, he said it had just been accepted, so he sent me a copy. I didn't even need to read it. Not with a recommendation like that coming from him."

My hand was trembling when I hung up the phone. Horrigan had not only gotten Monica appointed to study section, but he'd also known when her paper had been accepted. Which contradicted what the journal's managing editor had said when she told me earlier that he'd been shocked to learn that Monica's paper had been published by mistake.

I wasn't much of a sports fan, that was more Karen's thing. But I understood the saying, *Three strikes and you're out*.

And I counted four strikes against Emil Horrigan.

CHAPTER 37

took Karen through a summary of the day's events over drinks that evening. When I finished, she took a sip of wine and stared at me like she thought the story was crazy.

"Do you think I have it wrong? You look like you think I've lost it."

She shook her head as if to clear it. "No, sorry. It's hard to believe, but you've got it nailed. Any doubt that it was Horrigan is settled by his having told the NIH administrator to get Monica on the review panel before the paper was even published."

I wiped my brow in mock relief. "Phew! You had me worried for a minute."

She smiled. "I still don't get the underlying motive though. Why would a guy like Horrigan do all this to get a job that's pretty much the same as what he already has?"

"I know. I don't get that piece either. The only thing I can imagine is that he's in some kind of serious trouble at Harvard. Under investigation for fraud or sexual harassment, something of that nature."

Karen finished my thought. "And taking a job elsewhere would get him out of whatever mess he's in before it goes public. That could be, we've dealt with cases like that before. But I thought the way universities handled things had improved recently. Wouldn't Harvard inform Yale before he was hired?"

"Probably not if it was an ongoing inquiry. And I'm afraid that signing nondisclosure agreements and passing the harasser from one institution to another is still the way most of these cases are concluded. But I'm sure you'll be able to get to the bottom of it during your investigation."

"You mean as part of a murder investigation? I'm sure I could, except that we don't have enough evidence to launch one."

I almost choked on my scotch. "What do you mean? You just said you were convinced that I had it right."

"I am. But I'm not the one who needs to be convinced. If we moved against Horrigan, his lawyers would argue that all he did was try to boost a talented young woman's career by accepting her paper and getting her a spot as a grant reviewer. Everything else that happened was terrible, they'd say, but Horrigan didn't have anything to do with it. The job at Yale wasn't even particularly important to him; he just let himself be considered to see what would happen. And maybe to have a little extra ammunition to use in negotiating with Harvard about resources for his research center."

I was incredulous. "And you think a jury would believe that horseshit?"

"If it ever went that far, I bet at least some jurors would accept it as grounds for reasonable doubt, and we wouldn't get a conviction. But I can't imagine finding an ADA who would even want to prosecute the case. Not against a defendant like Horrigan."

"What happened to everyone being equal in the eyes of the law?"

She rolled her eyes. "Let's just say that some are still more equal than others. To move against someone of Horrigan's stature, we'd need direct evidence linking him to the murders. Without that, all we have is speculation."

An idea had started to come together in my head as Karen was speaking. I was going to let it percolate for a while, but something must have shown on my face because Karen gave me a searching look.

"What are you thinking? You have that look you get when you're coming up with some new cockamamie scheme."

I took another sip of scotch to stall while I thought about it a bit more. Then I told her.

When I finished, she just kept looking at me and shaking her head. "That may be the craziest damn thing I ever heard of. I know I've come up with some wild ones, but this sure as shit takes the cake."

"Does that mean you want to give it a shot?"

She laughed. "Sure, why not? I can't think of anything better. Let's just hope we're not the ones who get shot."

"Good." I drained my glass and got up. "I better go call Martin before he screws it all up."

"Okay. I'll let the office know I'm going to be out for a couple of days. You realize that I won't be able to bring in any help or backup for something this whacky?"

"Figures. You cops are so limited by the formalities. Rules of evidence and stuff like that."

CHAPTER 38

Martin answered his phone on the third ring. "What's up Brad? It's not your usual time to call. Are you making plans for that dinner I owe you?"

"Business first, I'm afraid. Have you told Horrigan that Carolyn's turned down the job?"

"I tried. He made me promise to let him know as soon as there was a decision, so I called shortly after I got Carolyn's email. Turns out that he's away for a conference in Paris. I left a message asking him to call me when he gets back tomorrow."

"Good. Does anyone else know about her decision?" I asked. "Members of the search committee maybe?"

"No, I'm waiting until I talk to Horrigan and can give the committee the full picture. Hopefully, that Carolyn's turned us down but Horrigan's delighted to accept. Why are you interested in this?"

"Because I don't want you to let Horrigan know that Carolyn's turned you guys down. Instead, tell him that she got back to you saying that she's decided to take the job, but needs to delay her formal acceptance until the beginning of next week to give me time to break the news to our board of trustees. In the meantime, you thought he should know."

There was a moment of silence on Martin's end. Then he spoke in a voice filled with disbelief. "Are you nuts? You want me to tell Emil Horrigan that Carolyn's taking the job here, and then a few days later tell him that she's decided to turn it down and it's his after all? I can't do that, that's crazy. Why the hell are you asking such a thing?"

I'd expected that kind of resistance. Martin wouldn't want to lie to someone like Horrigan. Especially if he was later going to turn around and offer him the job after all.

Now I had some convincing to do.

"Martin, look, I know this seems screwy. But can you just trust me on it for a few days? It's better for you not to know yet. But if Karen and I are right, it'll be over soon, and I promise to explain it all then."

It again took a minute for Martin to respond. When he did, he sounded apologetic. "I can't, Brad. I'm sorry, but Horrigan's not someone I can jerk around like that. You're going to have to tell me what's going on if you want me to lie to him about this, and it better be good." He paused for a moment. "Wait a minute, you implied that Karen's involved. It's not something to do with the case we were talking about this afternoon, is it?"

I wasn't surprised that Martin had already come close to figuring it out. It had never been easy to put anything over on him. I bit the proverbial bullet and went ahead.

"All right Martin, you're not leaving me any choice. It's a long story, you ready?"

I went through it all, leaving nothing out. Martin listened quietly except for a few questions and some well-placed expletives until I finished. Then he exploded.

"Jesus Christ! Of course I'll feed your story to the son of a bitch. He should rot in hell. But your plan is crazy. It's going to get both you and Karen killed. Carolyn too."

"Not to worry. We'll be ready. Karen and I have been in situations like this before."

"You always were a goddamned cocky asshole," Martin stated flatly. "You don't even know how many of them will be coming at you. Crap! I'll meet you at Carolyn's house tomorrow afternoon."

"Whoa! What are you talking about? Karen's a pro, and I've gotten used to gunplay by now."

"Uh-huh. And have you forgotten that I spent two years with the Army Rangers in Iraq? I sure as hell haven't. Just tell Karen to bring some extra weapons for me."

———

I woke up the next morning to find a text from Martin, sent a little before four o'clock.

Horrigan just called me from de Gaulle airport before catching his flight back from Paris. Didn't seem to care what time it was here. I could picture the flames coming out of the bastard's ears when I fed him the story!

CHAPTER 39

texted Carolyn while we were having coffee, telling her to stay home this morning. Karen and I were coming over, and we'd explain when we got there. Then we went to Karen's headquarters to pick up guns and a supply of ammunition. That side trip was a bit of a diversion, so it was after eleven by the time we got to Kennebunkport.

Carolyn greeted us with a look that started out as curious but turned to baffled when she saw we had Rosie with us and were carrying overnight bags. "What's happening? I'm happy to see you and everything, but what's so pressing for us to talk about? And what's with Rosie and the suitcases?"

Karen gave her a hug. "We'll tell you all about it in a minute. But first, is there room for my car in the garage? We don't want it to be visible from the street."

Carolyn's eyes widened even further than they already were, but she opened the garage and waited while Karen moved the car inside. That done, the three of us sat in Carolyn's living room while Rosie and Molly, always the best of friends, started playing tug-of-war with one of Molly's chew toys. I never understood how that worked, since the Newfoundland was more than five times larger than the pug. Maybe

Molly was laid back enough to let Rosie hold her own, or maybe Rosie was just that tough.

Either way, they provided an entertaining sideshow while Karen and I took Carolyn through the full story of how we'd established Horrigan's guilt. It wasn't the first time Carolyn had been the target of a criminal conspiracy, and she wasn't totally shocked that he'd tried to set her up for plagiarism. Just appalled by the horrendous lengths he'd then gone to in an attempt to cover up his guilt. And baffled as to why he'd do any of it.

"I still don't see why he'd care so much about the job at Yale," she said. "It's not any different than his situation at Harvard. Yet he did such horrible things and put everything he has at risk. What for?"

"That's the one piece we haven't figured out," I acknowledged. "My best bet is that he's under investigation for some kind of serious problem at Harvard. He's afraid it's not going to go his way, and his only move is to get out before the investigation's concluded, leaving whatever it is behind him to be buried."

Carolyn frowned. "You think the job at Yale is just a way for him to escape? I don't know. I can't imagine what kind of major trouble someone like him could be in."

I was about to remind her that we'd seen big men fall before. Like Tom Carlson. But the doorbell interrupted us.

Karen spoke in a hushed voice. "Are you expecting anyone?"

Carolyn shook her head, and Karen asked her to go into the kitchen while we dealt with whoever was at the door. She started to protest, but then the bell rang again, followed by three loud knocks. Karen waved a hand insistently, and Carolyn got up to leave the room. When she was gone, Karen retrieved a Heckler & Koch HK45 pistol from her overnight bag and handed it to me. Then she took a second out of the holster she wore on her hip, and we went to greet our visitor.

Karen positioned herself on the left side of the door, while I looked cautiously through a gap between the door and the curtains on the right. I was relieved to see only one man. Tall, maybe six foot two, and wearing jeans with a tight black T-shirt that showed off muscular arms. His face was obscured by dark sunglasses and a baseball cap pulled down low over his forehead. He wasn't carrying a weapon, but I thought he had the look of someone to whom lethal force would come easily. Potentially dangerous, but nothing Karen and I couldn't handle.

I whispered, "Just one," and gave Karen a thumbs-up. She held up her gun with a questioning look, asking if he was armed. When I shook my head, she yanked the door open and stuck her weapon in the intruder's face. "Police! Hands up and get on the ground!"

The man raised his hands. But then he laughed and slowly removed his sunglasses. "Hi guys. Didn't mean to startle you."

"Martin, you son of a bitch!" I moved past Karen to engulf him in a bear hug. "We didn't expect you this early."

"Obviously not. But once Horrigan got me up in the middle of the night, I figured I might as well get started on the drive up here." He moved inside and kissed Karen on the cheek. "Karen, good to see you again. Even if the circumstances are a little odd."

Before Karen could say anything, Carolyn came back from the kitchen. Her mouth flopped open when she saw who it was. "Dean Dawson! What. . . ?"

"Hi, Carolyn. Didn't these two tell you I was coming? Sorry to bust in, but when Brad told me there was going to be a little party at your place, I didn't want to miss it."

Carolyn managed to speak even though her mouth was still gaping. "Will somebody please tell me what the hell's going on?"

Martin turned to me with a half-smile. "You haven't filled her in?"

"We've gone through what Horrigan did but haven't gotten to what we're planning yet," I told him. "Why don't we all sit down, and we can continue."

Carolyn sat on the couch, and Martin took a chair across from her. "Quite a story, isn't it? Does it all make sense to you?"

"I guess it does in its own twisted way," she said. "But I still don't understand why Horrigan wanted the job at your place so badly. What kind of mess could he have gotten himself into that made him so desperate to leave Harvard?"

"My first guess would be—" I started to say.

But Martin held up a hand. "No need to guess. I have some new information on that."

We all turned to him, and when he had the floor, he continued.

"That hole in the story bothered me too, so while I was driving up here, I called an old friend who's on the Harvard Board of Overseers. Brad, you probably remember her. Elaine Marshfield."

"How could I forget Elaine? You two were quite the hot ticket when we were in graduate school. I didn't realize you'd kept in touch."

"She got divorced a few years ago, and we've resumed our friendship."

I grinned and shook my head. "Martin, you old fox."

Almost simultaneously, Carolyn gasped, "Dean Dawson!"

He nearly blushed, although I didn't think that was part of Martin's repertoire. "No, not like that. We just have lunch together once in a while when we're in the same city."

I responded with a sarcastic, "Uh-huh," and Carolyn gave him an exaggerated eyeroll. Karen just laughed.

"Geez, you guys!" Martin exclaimed. "Give a fella a break. Anyway, I told her I'd heard that Horrigan was being investigated and wondered if it had reached the overseer's level."

For Carolyn's benefit, I explained, "The overseers are the top governing board at Harvard."

"I figured they'd get involved if there was a case against someone of Horrigan's stature," Martin continued. "Elaine was coy at first, said she couldn't comment on an investigation that might or might not be in progress. But when I told her that we were on the verge of offering him a job, she said she couldn't let that happen. Turns out that well over a dozen current and former students have brought charges of harassment and intimidation against him. Elaine said that the investigating committee found the accusations highly credible, and she, along with several of her colleagues on the board, are determined to see him thrown out and publicly humiliated."

"About what I expected," I said. "A last-ditch attempt to save his filthy ass."

Carolyn shook her head. "For which I guess he was willing to do absolutely anything. I've got it now." Then she turned to Martin with a grin. "But Dean Dawson, I have to say you're full of surprises this morning. Showing up at my house, the way you're dressed, pumping an old girlfriend for inside information. More like a secret agent than a dean."

Martin bowed his head. "Why thank you. I'm honored to shatter your stereotype of what we deans are like. But wait until you hear what we're planning to do next. Oh, and you better start calling me Martin."

CHAPTER 40

"Hang on a minute," Karen interrupted. "Before we get to that, Martin, let's move your car out of sight. There's room for three in your garage, right Carolyn?"

"Sure. You may just have to move some of the junk out of the empty bay. And while you're doing that, let me see what I can find for lunch."

Martin gave her a grateful smile. "Good idea. I was getting worried about starving to death before the fun starts."

By the time we got the garage organized and Martin's car relocated, Carolyn had a platter of cheeses, cold cuts, and French bread waiting for us on the kitchen island. We all loaded plates with our choices, selected sodas or bottled waters from the fridge, and returned to the living room.

While we ate, I told Carolyn how we'd set Horrigan up. And what we expected his reaction would be.

"Jesus Christ!" she burst out. "You mean the three of you are here to protect me and the kids? Are you crazy! Why don't you just have him arrested? Or at least have a bunch of cops here instead of you guys?"

"We don't have enough evidence," Karen explained. "Without

something that directly ties him to the murders, it's all speculation. His lawyers would laugh us out of court if we tried to arrest him. There isn't even a solid basis to justify bringing in men as backup at this point."

"Hence the setup," I said. "If we're lucky, we'll be able to take whoever comes alive and get them to implicate Horrigan. Even if we don't manage that, an attack on you at this point fits too well with the bait Martin planted for him to wriggle out of it."

Carolyn was looking back and forth between us, as if she expected one of us to start laughing and say it was a joke. When that didn't happen, she took a deep breath and plowed ahead. "All right, so I'm your tethered goat. What exactly are you expecting? And when?"

I reached over and put a hand on her arm. "We think Horrigan's going to send men to kill you before you can formally accept the position. Today's Friday, and Martin told him that you expected to do that by the beginning of next week. To be safe, he'll set it up for either tonight or tomorrow."

"Probably tonight," Karen said. "He won't want to wait until the last minute. I suspect it'll be three or four men, most likely around two or three in the morning."

"But you and the kids won't be here, of course," I hastened to add. "As soon as they get home from school, we'll get you guys set up in a nice hotel. They can spend the weekend with movies, a heated pool, and room service."

I wasn't sure how Carolyn would react to being told she was slated to be Horrigan's next victim. But I certainly didn't anticipate what she said next.

"And what, you think I'm going to leave the three of you here to face my assassins? With those two little pistols you've got? You're goddamned nuts!"

Karen gave her a reassuring smile. "Don't worry, I picked up an ample supply of guns and ammunition from headquarters before coming here. And we'll have the advantage of surprise. They're not going to be expecting us, but we'll be watching for them. You know this is the kind of thing I do for a living, and Brad's been in several scrapes with me. He can handle himself by now."

"And I'm a former Army Ranger," Martin hastened to add. "Some of the things I had to do back then probably wouldn't fit your image of Dean Dawson."

"My God! You people are serious, aren't you? Well, I'm not going to go hide in some hotel then."

I held up a hand. "Wait a minute, what are you saying? We need you and the kids someplace safe and out of the way."

"The kids, sure. I'll call Paul and have him take them for the weekend. He can pick them up after school, and they won't even have to know what's going on. But I'm not going anywhere," she insisted.

I started to protest again, but Carolyn stopped me before I could get the words out. "Brad, shut up. Four of us will be better than three, and I know how to shoot at least as well as you do. I grew up hunting with my father and was damn good at it. I still go out with him sometimes when I get up north to visit my folks."

I glanced over at Karen, hoping for her backing. But she was studying Carolyn's face so intently that she didn't notice me. And she must have seen something I was missing.

Instead of arguing, she nodded slowly. "Okay, welcome to the club. Can you handle a semi-automatic rifle?"

Carolyn shrugged. "I've never used one, but I can learn. I'm at least as smart as all the crazies who've used them for mass shootings."

Martin smiled. "I hope so. I've never offered an endowed chair to a mass shooter. But I have a suggestion. Since we're going to be up all night, why don't we get a few hours of sleep now?"

Karen and I voiced our agreement, and Carolyn offered to get us set up in guest rooms. "Let me just call my idiot ex-husband and arrange for him to take the kids first. Karen, I may need you to get on the line and give me some official police backing. I'll put the phone on speaker."

It took a little convincing for Carolyn to get whoever answered the phone to put the call through. When Paul finally picked up, he was furious at the interruption.

"What the hell do you want? I'm in the middle of something important."

Without going into details, Carolyn explained that there was an emergency situation, and the kids wouldn't be safe at home. She needed him to pick them up from school and keep them for the weekend.

I could have predicted his response. "Screw that, I've got other things to do. You're probably just bullshitting me anyway, so I'll take them while you go off somewhere with a new boyfriend."

Karen reached over and took the phone before Carolyn could answer him. "This is Lieutenant Richmond of the state police. Your ex-wife isn't bullshitting you. Your children aren't safe here until we resolve this situation."

"And who the hell are you, some friend playing along with Carolyn's game? Go screw yourself."

"I'm commanding officer of MCU-South. And I'm telling you that your children are in danger. If you can't take them, I'll need to bring in child services. But why don't you verify my identity first?"

Karen broke the connection and handed the phone back to Carolyn. A few minutes later, it buzzed with an incoming text. Carolyn looked at it, gave a sarcastic snort, and passed it back to Karen.

Please give my sincere apologies to Lieutenant Richmond. I'll be happy to pick the kids up and take care of them for the weekend.

"Such an asshole," I muttered as Carolyn grabbed some towels from a closet in the hall and led the way to our guest rooms.

CHAPTER 41

The room that Karen, Rosie, and I were in came equipped with a comfortable queen-size bed, an en suite full bath, and a large walk-in closet. Luxurious for a room that I imagined was seldom used. We hadn't seen Martin's room down the hall, but I suspected it was equally lavish.

We were sleeping soundly when there was a knock on the door and Carolyn came in. More than an hour before we planned to reconvene in the living room and figure out our strategy for tonight. She was pale and on the brink of tears.

"It's the kids." The tears started flowing. "I can't believe this!"

I jumped up and took her arm as Karen sat up with a start. "What's wrong?" she asked without missing a beat.

"Paul called. He started yelling at me because the kids weren't there when he went to school to pick them up. He assumed I'd gotten them and was furious at me for jerking him around." Her voice rose in hysterics. "Now I don't know where they are!"

"Wait, try to stay calm." Karen sounded soothing, although I was sure she shared my rising sense of panic. "Have you called the school?"

Carolyn took a deep breath and nodded. "A hospital orderly came to the office around two and said that I'd been in an accident. I'd be fine but I had a mild concussion and had been admitted so they could watch me overnight. He said that he was supposed to bring the kids to see me, and the stupid school let him take them. At first, I thought it was some kind of mix-up, and the hospital would call soon. But they haven't, and I'm getting worried."

"Naturally. Did you get the orderly's name and what hospital he was from?" I asked.

"They didn't have his name. But he was from Maine Health in Kennebunk."

I gave them a call. As I feared, they assured me that no orderly had been sent to retrieve anyone's children from school. If a situation requiring it ever did arise, their procedure was to ask the police to pick up the kids.

I felt like I was going to be sick. We'd been wrong about Horrigan's plan. Rather than coming after Carolyn, he'd kidnapped her kids.

I glanced over at Karen. Although I couldn't read her mind, I was sure that she had the same thought. She looked as horrified as I felt.

"Carolyn, I'm afraid there's another possibility." Karen spoke softly, still trying to be soothing. "Horrigan could have kidnapped them."

"Oh my God, no!"

The blood rushed from her face, and she would have fallen if I hadn't grabbed her. Fortunately, once I got her sitting down with her head between her knees, she gradually recovered. When she was finally able to breathe normally again, she asked the obvious questions.

"What do we do? Why would he want to hurt my kids?"

"I don't think he wants to hurt them," Karen replied. "He's planning to use them to pressure you into turning down the job at Yale after all."

"You'll probably hear from him before too long," I said. "He'll want you to write to Martin saying that you've decided to decline the position. He'll promise to return the kids after you do that."

Carolyn looked confused. "I'm sorry, I'm too upset to think straight. You think he's doing this instead of trying to kill me?"

"He probably thinks that killing you would look too suspicious. This isn't, as long as he's sure you won't tell anybody."

I didn't add that he'd probably kill her in the end anyway. He wouldn't be able to trust her not to go to the police afterward. But he'd have a better chance of getting away with it if she'd already withdrawn as a job candidate. Especially if he made it look like an accident.

"If he's using my kids like that, I swear I'll strangle the bastard!" Carolyn suddenly sat up straight and spoke in a loud, strong voice. The confusion and uncertainty seemed to have left her, and she'd become a lioness rising in defense of her cubs. Ready to take on any aggressor that threatened her children.

"You'll have to wait in line," Karen declared. "But first, we need to know what he's planning. Which means we have to wait for him to call. When would you normally have picked the kids up?"

"Three o'clock, when school's over. Paul called me just after that."

Karen looked at her watch. "About thirty minutes ago. We'll probably hear from Horrigan soon. He'll figure you're in a panic by now and will be vulnerable to being manipulated."

Carolyn turned pale again. "You think he's going to call? What do I tell him? I've got to get my kids back."

"He'll call all right," I assured her. "He needs to tell you what he wants you to do. When he does, put the phone on speaker so Karen and I can listen in and advise you on how to respond."

"It's important for him to think you're alone," Karen added. "We'll write notes for you on a pad of paper, so we won't have to say anything, and he won't know we're here. Sound okay?"

"As long as you can keep my kids safe, anything's okay."

"We will," I promised. "And at the same time, we're going to nail the bastard's ass."

CHAPTER 42

We went into the living room to wait for Horrigan's call. Martin had been awakened by all the activity, and the four of us sat around a coffee table that held Carolyn's phone along with pens and a pad of paper. It didn't take long.

Carolyn put her phone on speaker, and we heard a deep voice on the other end. "I've got your kids."

"I know. I've been expecting you to call."

"Do you know who this is?"

Karen nodded, and Carolyn said, "I assume you're Emil Horrigan."

"Good. I'm glad Yale didn't pass me over for someone too stupid to understand what's going on. Your kids are fine, and you can have them back unharmed. I just need you to send the dean a polite email declining the position. You can thank him for the offer and say that MTRI came up with such a surprisingly generous counter that you've decided to stay there after all."

Karen scribbled, *Then what?*

"And what happens then?" Carolyn asked. "Do you want me to bcc you on the email?"

I gave her a thumbs-up. That was a nice touch.

"No! Maybe you *are* stupid. Don't copy me on anything. The dean will call me soon enough when he gets your email. I'll let you know when and where you can pick up your kids after I hear from him."

I shook my head vigorously. Once she'd declined the job, Horrigan would have no reason to return the kids.

Karen must have reached the same conclusion. She held up a hand, signaling Carolyn not to respond yet. Then she scribbled rapidly. *Absolutely not! You have to get the kids back the same time as you send the email. A simultaneous exchange.*

Carolyn nodded and spoke firmly into the phone. "No. I need to see my kids before I email Dean Dawson. And I want them back at the same time."

Horrigan didn't answer immediately. When he finally responded, he did nothing to hide his anger. "Bitch! I should have known you'd be difficult. But all right, we'll do it your way. I'll meet you in the parking area of the Owl's Nest Wildlife Refuge in Kennebunk at six thirty. You know where it is?"

"I'll find it."

"Okay. Bring the email as a draft on your phone so you can send it from there. I'll have your kids with me, and you can take them once that's done. Come alone and don't say anything to anyone, especially not the cops. We'll be watching your house, and we'll have an eye out for anything that looks out of place at the refuge. If you screw around with us, you won't see your kids again."

He broke the connection, and Carolyn put the phone down. "Did I do okay?"

"Perfect," I assured her.

She took a deep breath. "What do we do now then? I guess I could do as he says, get my kids back, and you could arrest him afterward."

Karen, Martin, and I all shook our heads simultaneously. Then we let Karen answer. "We can't trust him. The one advantage we have is that he doesn't know the three of us are here. So, we can go to the exchange with you as backup."

"But the kids won't be safe if he sees you guys," Carolyn objected.

"Don't worry, he won't see us or spot anything amiss," I assured her. "We can get down behind the seats of your car while it's still in the garage, and all anybody who's watching will see is you driving to the meet by yourself."

"Is your car large enough?" Karen asked.

"Sure, it's a big Jeep SUV with three rows of seats. But what do you think he's planning?"

"We're going to have to wait and see," Karen said. "Maybe we'll be lucky, and it'll go down like he said. In that case, we can all just go home, and I'll have him picked up later. But I'm afraid there's a good chance he won't trust you not to go to the police once he gives you back the kids."

Carolyn blanched. "You think he'll try to keep them for security?"

Karen kept her voice soft and gentle. "That's one possibility. But he might also fall back on his original plan of killing you once you've turned down the job. Maybe making it look like an accident."

I nodded grimly. "Those are the moves we need to be ready for. And he'll probably have his men with him."

Carolyn looked at each of us in turn, as if she wanted to see whether we were all in agreement. Then she sighed heavily. "So we could be going into the same kind of firefight you were anticipating here. And Horrigan has even more of an edge, since he has my kids."

"The advantage isn't all on his side, though. You have the element of surprise on yours," I pointed out.

"The three of us," Martin hastened to add. "Locked and loaded, right Karen?"

She nodded agreement and got up from the couch. "Let's go out to the garage, and you can see the weapons collection I brought."

———

We made a first stop to check out Carolyn's SUV. "Perfect, even dark tinted windows," Karen commented. "I'll lie down between the first and second row, Brad between the second and third, and Martin you take the cargo space. Carolyn can cover us with blankets or something, and she'll be the only person they'll be able to see."

"How about when we get there?" Martin asked. "If Horrigan or his men come over to the car, we'll look suspicious."

"Right, but that doesn't have to happen," Karen said. "Carolyn, we'll need you to get out and walk away from the car to talk to them. Is that okay?"

"Sure. But how will you guys know what's happening?"

"We're going to set up a two-way communication system that'll let us hear everything going on. It's one of the goodies I brought from MCU headquarters. Let me show you."

We followed Karen to the rear of her Volvo, where she opened the cargo compartment and removed a small plastic bag. Then she handed Carolyn a miniature flesh-colored earpiece, no bigger than a quarter inch, and a rectangular box that was about half the size of a cell phone.

"This is the modern version of having you wear a wire," she explained. "The box will receive transmissions from my phone and relay the signal to your earpiece. It'll also pick up anything you say, or whatever's said by anyone around you, and transmit those signals back to me. We'll hear everything that's going on and be ready to jump in if you need us."

Carolyn put the transmitter in her pocket and the earpiece in her left ear. "Got it."

"Okay. While we're here, I may as well distribute the rest." Karen reached into the car again and came out with two pistols. One was an HK45, the same gun Karen and I were already carrying, which she gave to Martin. The second was a Glock 42, which she handed to Carolyn, noting that it was about half the size of the HK and would be easy to hide in a pocket. Next were AR-15 style semi-automatic rifles for Martin, Karen, and me. Martin received his with a smile, while Karen explained apologetically that a rifle would be impossible for Carolyn to conceal when she got out of the car.

Four Kevlar vests came next. Martin and I put ours on, but Carolyn looked puzzled. "How can I wear this? They'll be able to see it if I get out of the car to talk to them."

Karen smiled gently. "Underneath your shirt. They can be worn either inside or outside of other clothing. Bullet-proof either way."

Carolyn rolled her eyes. "Stupid me. Okay, what's next?"

"Now we get ready to go," Karen took out some zip tie handcuffs and closed the back of her car. "Get your email to Martin written and save it in your draft folder so it's all set to send. Then we'll establish the connection between my phone and your transmitter. After that, we go to this refuge place and hope for the best."

CHAPTER 43

The entrance to the wildlife refuge was marked by a metal gate with a sign saying it closed at five o'clock. I wondered how we were going to get in until Carolyn got out of the car and found that the padlock securing the gate had been broken. Presumably Horrigan or his men wanted to make sure that nothing interfered with our meeting.

We drove down a dirt road to a parking area in the middle of a pine forest. It had been cleared of all but a half-dozen remaining trees and was large enough for thirty or so cars. But the only vehicle parked there now was a large white van in the center of the lot.

"Park over on the right near the edge of the woods," Karen directed. "That'll put us about twenty yards from the van, which must be where they're waiting with the kids. Then you can get out and start walking over to it. We'll be able to see what's going on through your tinted windows."

A moment after Carolyn got out, a tall man with a brown ponytail exited the passenger side of the van and started walking over to her. They met in the middle, near one of the trees that had been left standing, and we could hear him ask Carolyn for her phone.

"Wait a minute," she objected. "You're not Emil Horrigan. What's going on?"

He gave a snide laugh. "No, I'm not Horrigan. He's in the van with your kids, waiting for me to show him the email you're going to send. If he approves, I'll bring your kids back with me."

"No. Show me my kids first," Carolyn demanded.

"Damn it! Do as you're told, or I'll be showing you their dead bodies." He held out a hand. "Give me the damned phone. Now."

Karen hurriedly transmitted, "Not much choice. Give it to him."

"All right." Carolyn handed him her phone, and he told her to stay where she was while he went back to the van.

We waited impatiently for several minutes. Then Martin's phone buzzed. He looked at it and nodded. "I just got Carolyn's email. They must have sent it from the van."

A moment later, a solitary figure exited the van and started walking back toward Carolyn.

"He's alone!" Carolyn's voice over the transmitter sounded close to panic. "Now what do I do? Where the hell are my children?"

"Take it easy, stay in control." Karen spoke softly, trying to calm her. "Something's fishy. They already sent the email. Maybe they didn't even bring the kids with them. Stay cool and try to get him to tell you what's going on."

When Ponytail had covered half the distance between them, Carolyn yelled out, "Where are my children? What the hell's going on?"

He held up a hand. "Don't worry. Horrigan approved your email, and we already sent it. He has your kids nearby, and I'm going to take you to them. Then you can all go home." He gestured to Carolyn's car. "Come on, you can drive. It's not far."

"No! You've been lying to me from the beginning. I want to see who's in the goddamned van for myself," Carolyn insisted. "No more games."

She started to move toward the van, but Ponytail grabbed her arm. "No, damn it! I already said, your car. Now move!"

"It's okay," Karen said hastily. "Come back here, and we'll take care of him."

Except Carolyn had gone into panic mode and wasn't listening anymore. She twisted sideways to free her arm and kicked Ponytail in the side of his knee. As he stumbled and fell, she started to run around him toward the van.

Unfortunately, he was too fast for her. He grabbed her left ankle, and she went down with a scream. I wasn't sure if it was pain or anger. Perhaps both.

She recovered and got back on her feet quickly. But he was quicker. By the time she was upright, he was standing in front of her with a gun in his hand. Pointed at her chest.

"Last chance, bitch. Turn around and walk to your car."

"Do it!" Karen urged.

But Carolyn just screamed, "No!" and started toward the van again.

We watched helplessly as he pulled the trigger, and Carolyn fell to the ground. He started over to her, presumably to finish the job if she was still alive.

Except Martin reacted first. With a yell of, "Bastard shot her!" he rammed his rifle through the window and let fly a series of shots in rapid succession.

Ponytail, or his body, jerked back and forth as the bullets struck. Then his remains fell to the ground in a heap.

"Got the piece of shit!" Martin exclaimed. Turning toward the door, he added, "Cover me, I'm going out to get Carolyn."

But before Martin could make his move, two men jumped out of the van, rolled underneath it, and opened fire with automatic rifles. Our car shook from the barrage of bullets as it was being torn apart with us inside.

CHAPTER 44

"We have to get out of here, the car won't protect us," Karen yelled. "Are you guys okay?"

"So far," I choked out. Martin just grunted.

"Let's move then. Stay low and roll out of the right-hand doors. Then crawl on your bellies into the forest. There are some big boulders scattered around, and we can take cover behind one of them. Then we'll plan our next moves."

"Wait, we can't leave Carolyn behind!" Martin protested.

I couldn't see Karen's face, but I knew how much she liked being countermanded in this kind of situation. I anticipated an angry retort, but she controlled her temper.

"We won't, don't worry. But we have to get out of here before we're shredded. Then we'll talk, but let's move while we can!"

With that, Karen rolled out of the car and started crawling into the woods. Martin and I followed, while the shooters continued firing at the car. At some point, they must have realized that we'd abandoned it, because they started shooting into the woods instead. But by then, the three of us were crouched behind a large boulder about six feet past the forest's edge. Safe, at least for the moment.

Martin must have guessed that Karen hadn't appreciated his earlier outburst and felt the need to apologize. "I'm sorry I questioned you back there, Karen. I know you wouldn't abandon her."

Karen managed a smile despite our circumstances. "Thanks. And I think I have a way to get to her safely." She was suddenly interrupted by a volley of rifle fire striking our boulder. I was afraid they'd found us, but the shots quickly moved off to our left.

"They're just exploring," Karen said. "They know we're back here somewhere, but not exactly where. So, here's what I'm thinking. Martin, do you remember the fire and move tactic from your Ranger days?"

"Sure. One of our basic combat maneuvers."

"Good. That's what you and I are going to do. The goal is to work our way around the edge of the forest to the far side of the van. We'll draw their fire as we go, in the end leaving Brad at their backs. Once that's accomplished, Brad, you should be able to safely go to Carolyn. I don't know what you'll find. All we can do is hope she's alive."

I exhaled slowly. It seemed like a vain hope after she'd been shot at close range. *Unless*, I dared to think, *the bullet-proof vest had worked.* "Okay. I'll do whatever I can for her."

"Be sure to stay low and don't make any noise," Karen cautioned. "If they see or hear you, we're screwed. It looks like she's near a tree that should give you some cover when you get to her. And Martin and I will maintain a constant barrage of fire, so hopefully we'll be able to hold their attention."

"Got it. And what should I do after taking care of Carolyn?"

"Move back to the edge of the forest and get behind one of the big boulders. Then you open fire, from what will be behind them. We'll have them pinned between us, and they won't know there's only one of you. With any luck, they'll think they're surrounded and throw in the towel."

"Good plan!" Martin enthused. "And if they don't surrender, we can move in and squeeze them while Brad keeps firing from behind."

"Exactly," Karen said. "Now let's go. Martin, you move out first. I'll cover you."

Martin started running to the right, angling a bit deeper into the woods. As soon as he was clear, Karen opened fire on the van with a continuous barrage of bullets that kept them pinned down. That continued for a few minutes, until we heard shots coming from a new position to our right. Martin had reached his first stop and was now providing cover for Karen's run.

Karen stopped firing, and the two men under the van started shooting in Martin's direction, targeting the new source that had them under assault. Karen gave me a quick kiss and began her run, angling somewhat deeper into the woods than Martin so that she stayed out of the line of fire. I watched her for a bit until she was out of sight. But I knew she'd made it safely when shots started coming from a new direction, somewhere behind Martin.

That was Martin's signal to stop firing and move again. And when shots started coming from someplace farther around the perimeter, Karen ceased firing and was on the move to her next station.

The two of them operated like a well-practiced team, even though they'd never done this maneuver before. At least not together. But before long, their movements stopped, and the assault on the van was coming from two locations on the opposite side of the parking area. Horrigan's men had turned in that direction and had their hands full exchanging fire with Karen and Martin. I was safely out of their line of vision.

My turn had come.

CHAPTER 45

started toward Carolyn, more worried about what I'd find when I got to her than about being shot myself. She was lying midway between the van and her car, and I crawled carefully on my stomach across the ten yards or so it took to reach her from the edge of the forest. Fortunately, Karen and Martin seemed to have the two shooters fully occupied, and I made it across the parking area without being spotted.

Carolyn was lying on her back, as she would have fallen after being shot in the chest. Not a good sign. But when I got closer, I realized that something was off. *There was no blood.*

I moved to her side as fast as I could crawl. When I had almost reached her, I heard her speak softly.

"Brad, stay down and keep quiet. I'm okay. The vest must have worked. I felt the bullet hit my chest, and the impact knocked me over. I could see the prick who shot me coming over with his gun pointed at me, ready for the coup de grace, but one of you guys got him in time."

"That was Martin. He reacted instantaneously." I kept my voice low.

She managed a weak grin. "A fast-shooting dean. Interesting. Anyway, I was about to get up, but two guys jumped out of the van and started shooting in this direction. I stayed put so they'd think I was dead, but I'm fine. Just sore where the bullet hit me."

I almost jumped up and down with relief. But instead, I crawled behind the tree she was lying next to, giving us both some protection from the shooters under the van. "Thank God you're okay. Let me have a look."

When I opened her shirt, I could see the bullet trapped in the vest. It would have gone through to her heart if the vest hadn't stopped it, but the only damage I could find was a large bruise underneath. "You've got a big bruise that I'm sure is going to hurt for a while. But the bullet didn't penetrate. We'll get you checked for any internal damage the impact may have caused when we get out of here, but you'll be fine."

"And how're we going to do that? Get out of here, I mean."

I told her the plan, adding that she should stay where she was. She started to argue, but when I pointed out that she couldn't contribute any useful firepower without a rifle, she reluctantly agreed to stay put.

The two thugs under the van were still busy shooting at Karen and Martin, so I decided it would be safe to make a quick run to the boulder on the edge of the forest that I was going to use for cover. Maybe I was overconfident after finding Carolyn alive, but not to have crawled was a stupid mistake. Just before I reached the boulder, I heard a bullet whiz by. When I turned to look at the van, I could see that one of the shooters was no longer firing into the woods at Karen and Martin. Instead, I'd become his target.

I dove and rolled behind the boulder just as it was struck by a flurry of bullets. I was safe for now, but I'd blown Karen's plan. They knew I was here, and they'd seen that there was just one of me. Karen's intended bluff that they were surrounded by reinforcements would no longer work.

I was struggling to come up with an alternative strategy when I realized that the pattern of shots from the van had changed. There was only one man now, firing into the woods at Karen and Martin. The one who'd been shooting at me was gone. Maybe he'd exposed himself, and one of them had gotten him from the rear. But whatever had happened, it looked like the odds had shifted in our favor. With three of us to one of them, maybe Karen could talk the remaining shooter into surrendering after all.

I resumed firing at the van, waiting for Karen to make her play. But instead, a voice I didn't recognize spoke from behind me. "Having fun there, buddy?"

I turned to see a man pointing a rifle at me with his finger on the trigger. A hollow sensation grew in my chest as I realized this was the missing shooter. He hadn't been shot but had left the van to circle behind me. And now he was enjoying a moment's amusement by taunting me before he finished me off.

If I prayed, this would be a good time. But I didn't, so my thoughts turned to Karen while I waited for the bullet to come. We should have had more time together. She was strong, a survivor, but I knew my loss would hit her hard, just like hers would hit me if the situation was reversed.

The shot came without warning. But it wasn't from Horrigan's thug. Instead, it was from in back of him. Three shots actually, which struck him in the back and tore open his chest in a way that left no doubt as to his fate.

Then Carolyn came out of the woods, holding the pistol that Karen had given her in the garage. "Karen was right," she said. "This may be small, but it works just fine."

"How . . . how did you. . . ?" I stammered, trying to bring myself back to a new reality.

She smiled. "I saw him sneaking around behind you and figured it was time to get off my ass. I made a circle of my own, and well, you see the results. Thank God I was in time."

"Thank *you*. I'm glad you remembered how to shoot."

"Like riding a bike, I guess. But hitting him from this close didn't take much of a shot." She motioned toward the van, where the remaining thug was exchanging fire with Karen and Martin. "Should we get back to dealing with that one?" Picking up the dead man's rifle, she added, "I can use this and join you."

I was about to agree, until I realized there was a way I could let Karen and Martin know what had happened. And initiate the next part of Karen's strategy at the same time.

"Hang on a minute. I want to send him a message first, as well as letting Karen and Martin know that we're both okay."

Then I shouted at the van. "Police! Throw down your weapon. Your partner's dead and there are four of us, two on each side of you. You're finished."

To emphasize the point, I signaled Carolyn to move a few yards to the right. Then we each fired several rounds toward the van, making sure the shooter could tell that there were two of us back here. When we stopped, Karen and Martin repeated the show from the other side.

Then Karen issued another warning. "This is Lieutenant Richmond. You're boxed in, and there's no way out. Throw down your weapon and come out with your hands up. You don't have to die today."

There was no response, and after a brief interval, Karen tried again. "This is your last chance. If you don't comply, we'll resume firing in thirty seconds."

This time, the rifle came flying out from underneath the van. It was followed by the shooter, hands raised above his head.

CHAPTER 46

We kept our weapons ready as all four of us converged on Horrigan's thug, a burly redhead with a bushy, unkempt beard. Karen and Martin reached him first, and Carolyn ran to the van, hoping her kids were there. I followed her, but it only took a quick look to see that the van was empty.

"I can't say I'm surprised," Karen said when we rejoined her and Martin. "It makes sense that Horrigan would have the kids somewhere else." Motioning toward the captured shooter with her head, she added, "Now we just have to get this piece of shit to tell us where."

Then she used her rifle to prod the prisoner, who was already in handcuffs, toward the van. "Sit on the ground over there, back to the rear wheel." When he complied, she used a second pair of handcuffs to secure his hands to a wheel spoke. "All right, asshole, that should hold you. Now I need you to talk. What's your name?"

He spat on the ground instead of answering.

Karen shrugged. "Okay, we'll do this the hard way. Brad, would you mind shooting this bastard in the leg?"

I knew how this worked. We'd played it through before. "Sure, no problem. Fella, do you care which one?"

He paled as I raised my gun. "No preference? All right, I'll do your left first."

"No, wait!" he screamed. "I'll talk. It's Jim. Jim Dorn."

That was quick, I thought. *I didn't even need to fire a warning shot.* "Should I shoot him anyway?" I asked Karen. "He was kinda slow."

She seemed to take a minute to think about it. "Maybe not yet. Let's see how he does with the rest of my questions."

"Anything! I'll tell you whatever I know. Just don't let him shoot me."

I lowered the gun. Poor Jim Dorn had been reduced to a trembling ball of fear.

"We'll see," Karen replied. "Who hired you?"

"The first guy you shot. The one with the ponytail. He was in charge. His name was Gary something."

Karen shook her head. "That's not what I want. And I think you know it. Brad, can you help Jim here focus?"

"Of course."

I raised the gun again, and Jim screamed. "No! Wait. What are you asking?"

"I'm asking who hired you three clowns for this operation, moron."

"I don't know. Some guy hired Gary to put together a crew. I never met him."

"You're going to have to do better than that. Brad. . . ."

This time I fired a shot that landed a few inches to the left of his knee. He screamed again. "Stop! I don't know his name, I swear. Gary just said he was some kind of big ass professor. I remember he said he'd never have figured a college professor would order a job like this."

Karen nodded. "Okay, you're doing better. But stay focused. You only get one warning shot. Right, Brad?"

I grinned at the man on the ground. "That's right, chief. Just the one."

"Clear, Jim?" Karen asked. "Now, why don't you go ahead and tell me the plan. Did you three take the kids from school?"

"No, some other guys picked them up. Our job was just to meet the woman here." Looking at Carolyn, he added, "Her."

"Then what? Don't make this like pulling teeth."

"She was supposed to have some kind of message on her phone. Gary was going to get the phone and send the message to the boss. If he said it was okay, we were going to send it from her phone to wherever it was supposed to go."

I raised my gun to his head. "And then?"

He licked his lips. "Gary was supposed to kill her. Look, it wasn't my idea! I didn't want to do it!"

I lowered the gun again.

"All right," Karen said. "As long as you tell us the truth, I won't let him shoot you. We saw Gary take her phone and go back to the van. What happened after that?"

"He sent a copy of her message to the boss. I guess the boss approved it, because Gary sent it on after that. Then he came back out here for her, but you guys shot him."

"And what about the kids?" I asked. "Are they somewhere nearby?"

"They're with the boss. Gary was supposed to text him when we were done with the woman. Then we were going to go and get them."

"And do what? Were you going to kill them, too?" Karen demanded.

He looked even more terrified. "It wasn't me! I said I didn't want to kill no kids, but Gary said we didn't have a choice. We were supposed to send the car off a cliff with them and her in it. Gary said it would look like an accident, and nobody'd know they'd been shot after it had all burned up."

He must have thought that admission would seal his fate. His eyes were wide with fear as he looked back and forth between us, pleading incoherently for his life.

Karen made him sweat for a bit to see if anything more would come out. Then she let him off the hook. "All right. You've told us, and I promised we wouldn't shoot you. Just one more question. Where do we find your boss and the kids?"

"I don't know. The only thing I can tell you is that Gary said the boss had them not far from here, in a big house on the ocean."

"Okay. I'm going to have a couple of my men come and get you.

You'll spend the night in jail, and several years after that. But you'll live to see tomorrow."

Karen gestured for me to follow her, and we moved a few yards away from the prisoner. He wasn't going anywhere.

Carolyn and Martin were just behind us, and I was surprised to see that she was holding his hand. Maybe she needed the reassurance of physical contact after hearing what was intended for her children, but I hadn't seen anything like that kind of warmth between them before.

Then I realized that everything was different now. I'd told her that Martin's quick action had saved her life. And that had forged a new and unbreakable connection between them. I wondered where it might lead.

I mentally shook myself to return to the matter at hand. "How about I go and get dead Gary's phone?" I suggested. "There must be texts between him and Horrigan, and I can send something to tell Horrigan that we're set here and coming to his place soon."

"Good idea, he'll be expecting a message like that," Karen agreed. "In the meantime, I'm going to call headquarters. It shouldn't be hard to figure out where Horrigan's house on the coast is, and they can send a squad there to get the kids and pick him up. I'll have them send another unit here to take Jim in, as well as someone to pick up the dead guys." Turning around, she added, "Carolyn, I'm afraid your car's not going anywhere, so I'll also get transportation for you and Martin back to your house."

"No way!" Carolyn was emphatic. "I need to go to Horrigan's and get my children. I'm not going back home to sit and wait. What are you and Brad going to do?"

"We'll have a car take us to Horrigan's and meet the others there."

"Then it can take me too," Carolyn insisted.

"And me," Martin declared. "I'm sticking with this."

Carolyn looked up at him with a glow of warmth in her eyes. "Thanks, mister fast-shooting dean." Then she turned back to Karen. "Anyway, who knows what Horrigan might do if a bunch of cops show up at his house. We can't risk that."

She has a good point, I thought. And both she and Martin had shown they were assets in a fight. I wasn't surprised by Martin, given his military experience. But it wasn't something I'd expected from Carolyn. She even seemed unfazed after shooting a man for what, I assumed, was her first time. A mother's instinct to protect her children appeared to have overridden all else.

I was about to second Carolyn's suggestion, but Karen held up her hands in surrender. "Okay, I hear you. And you're right that a bunch of cops going in could be risky. How about the four of us take the van to Horrigan's? That's the vehicle they'll be expecting, and after this I'm sure we can handle whatever sort of fight they try to put up. I'll have a team meet us there as backup, but we'll go in first."

Relief showed all over Carolyn's face. "Thank you. After what he was planning for my kids, I want to be there to see the bastard go down."

———

I went over to Gary's corpse while Karen called MCU headquarters. His phone was in one of his front pockets, same place as I kept mine. It was locked, but I was able to open it with touch ID using his thumb. A little macabre, but effective.

His last text had gone out at 6:43. Shortly after we'd arrived in the parking area.

Got the woman's phone. Has email draft. Forwarding to you now.

Horrigan had replied a few minutes later.

Her email's fine, go ahead and send it. Then take care of her and come get the damn kids.

I looked back over earlier messages to see if they had a similar tone. Those from Gary all sounded pretty much the same, so I sent Horrigan a new message.

Sent email and woman taken care of. On way to your place now.

Then I pocketed the phone. It would be good to have in case Horrigan replied. As well as making one more addition to the pile of evidence against him.

And one of his earlier messages had given Gary his address, so we didn't need to wait for Karen's guys to track it down.

CHAPTER 47

y the time I rejoined the group, the prisoner had been released from the van and secured to the remains of Carolyn's car. Karen was on her phone to MCU, and I heard her describing the locations of the two dead men. Then she thanked whoever was on the line and ended the call.

"All set. They'll pick up Jim and the two corpses. As soon as they figure out what property Horrigan owns in Maine and send me the address, we're good to go."

I showed her Gary's phone. "No need to wait. Horrigan was kind enough to text that himself."

She looked at it and nodded. "How considerate of him. Okay, let's go. Brad, you drive, and Martin, you ride shotgun. Or automatic rifle, as it were. Carolyn and I will get in the back so we can duck down out of sight if anyone meets the car."

The address Horrigan had sent turned out to be on the Nubble Peninsula in York, about five miles south of the Cliff House, where I'd gone for the trustees' meeting about Carolyn's retention. When we got there, we found a spacious contemporary-style house that, like the Cliff House, was mounted on a rocky bluff above the ocean. No doubt, it offered similarly spectacular views.

Two burly men wearing sports coats were waiting at the front door. From the bulges underneath, it wasn't hard to tell that their jackets were worn to conceal weapons.

Martin and I got out of the van carefully, our own guns within easy reach in the small of our backs.

One of the men held up a hand. "Hold it right there. Who are you guys?"

"Gary and Jim," I replied. "The boss is expecting us."

"Uh-huh. And where's Mike? There's supposed to be three of you."

"He's behind us. Driving the woman's car with her body in it, so we'll be ready to send it over a cliff when we get the kids." I faked a snide laugh. "It moves a little slow now, took a couple of bullets back there in the parking lot."

He grunted his understanding. "Okay. We'll take you in to see the boss, and then you can get the kids. Just have to frisk you first."

Martin and I exchanged a quick glance. *Should we surrender our guns? Or should we take these two now?*

Karen made the decision for us. She threw the car door open and jumped out, pointing her gun at the one who'd been doing the talking. "Police! Hands up!" He complied, but thug number two apparently thought he had an opening. He started to raise his hands, but then plunged his right hand under his coat. I was about to jump him, except Karen was quicker. She turned on him before he could get his gun out, her own weapon in hand. "You too, asshole. Hands behind your head, unless you want to see how fast I can pull the trigger."

That was apparently enough. He blanched and did as ordered.

"All right. Brad, can you get their guns?"

Martin joined Karen in keeping them covered while I got the weapons from under their coats and patted them down. Nothing besides the guns that had been in their shoulder holsters.

Karen cuffed both thugs' hands behind their backs, bound their legs, and secured them to the van. Then she stepped back and admired her handiwork. "I think you boys should be okay here for now. Where do we find Horrigan and the children?"

Neither of them responded, and I was about to start threatening them, like I'd handled Jim back in the parking lot. But Carolyn apparently decided she wanted that role for herself. She put a restraining hand on my arm and turned to Karen. "Mind if I help with these two?"

Karen shrugged. "Sure, why not?"

Carolyn stepped forward, eyes flashing with anger, and put her gun against thug number one's head. "Are you one of the assholes that kidnapped my children?"

He turned pale and started trembling. "We only did what we was told! We didn't want to hurt no kids! They're fine, they're just in the house."

"Where in the house?" Karen asked. "Quick, or I'll let her shoot you."

"I don't know! One of the bedrooms, I guess. Harry's with them. He took them in and asked the boss where to put them."

"All right. Where do we find the boss?"

"He's in his study. It's on the first floor toward the back."

"Anybody else in the house?"

He shook his head. "No, there's just the three of us that brought the kids here. Boss sent all the regular staff away so they wouldn't see nothing."

Karen nodded and turned to Carolyn. "That's all I need. They're all yours now."

Carolyn raised the gun to his head, and the thug screamed in terror. "No! Please! I've told you everything. Don't kill me!"

Carolyn turned to Karen. "You don't care if I go ahead and shoot them?"

Karen shrugged amicably. "Whatever you want to do is fine with me."

Carolyn started moving her gun back and forth between them, a blood-chilling smile on her face. By now, they were both pleading for their lives, and a dark stain was spreading across the second thug's crotch. Then she lowered the weapon.

"What the hell, I can kill them later. Let's go get my kids first."

CHAPTER 48

Karen flung the front door open, and the four of us burst into the house with our weapons at the ready. Only to find ourselves in an empty room. The oversized living room featured comfortable-looking coastal-style furniture and floor-to-ceiling windows looking out over the ocean. A French door led to a dining room, with another floor-to-ceiling window on its back wall, and I imagined, a connection to the kitchen somewhere to the right. A second door on the right side of the living room led to a hallway and a staircase to the upper level. Without speaking, Karen signaled that Martin and I should go through to the dining room while she and Carolyn investigated the hallway.

The dining room was furnished in the same style as the living room and was equally empty. It connected to a kitchen outfitted with marble counter tops and high-end stainless-steel appliances. But again, no people. Another door out of the kitchen led to the hallway we'd seen from the living room, where Karen and Carolyn were waiting for us.

I addressed Karen in a hushed voice. "All clear behind us."

"Same here so far. The door between us and the staircase is a bath-room. Then there are three rooms on the other side of the stairs. I'm betting Horrigan's office is the door closest to us, so it can wrap around the kitchen for an ocean view."

"Sounds right. Shall we go in?"

She nodded. "But quietly. We don't want to give ourselves away if he's not in there."

Putting a finger to her lips to signal Martin and Carolyn, she carefully opened the door. We were greeted by the back of a man with short gray hair, sitting in front of a six-foot computer desk that looked out at the ocean from the rear of the room. He was intently focused on the computer and hadn't heard us enter.

Karen motioned for us to lower our guns and holstered her own weapon as we proceeded into the room. Then she announced our presence in a louder than usual voice.

"Emil Horrigan?"

He swiveled around in his chair, mouth open and eyes wide. "Who the hell are you?!"

Karen held up her badge. "Lieutenant Richmond, Maine State Police. You're under arrest for the murder of George Evans, the attempted murder of Carolyn Gelman, and the kidnappings of Gail and Robert Gelman. Massachusetts will no doubt add charges for the murders of Monica Kushman and Leonard Frankel. Stand up and put your hands behind your back."

Horrigan stared at her in shock. Then he closed his mouth and emitted a mocking laugh. "What are you, crazy? Look at the four of you, you're not cops. You look like you've spent the day playing football in the mud. What'd you do, order the badge on Amazon?"

I had to admit, he had a point. We were all a mess, and there wasn't a uniform among us. Nor anything resembling the coat and tie generally worn by Boston detectives.

I was pretty sure Karen had never encountered this particular kind of resistance before, but she seemed unfazed as she drew her pistol and pointed it at him. "Do as I say. Now!"

He gave the derisive laugh again. "If you are a cop, you're not going to shoot me. Do the other three have toy badges too?"

He started running his eyes over the three of us in turn. I'd spoken with him a few times at conferences, but he didn't seem to recognize me. I wasn't sure if he'd ever met Carolyn, and she only got a quick glance. But when he came to Martin, I could see recognition dawn. He furrowed his brow, and then burst out, "Wait a minute! You're the dean from Yale!"

Then he returned his gaze to Carolyn. "And you're the Gelman woman. What the hell is going on here?"

"What's going on is that you're under arrest." Karen had pulled out her identification card and shoved it in his face. "Amazon doesn't sell these, asshole. Now get up or I'll drag you out of that chair."

He looked at the ID, taking time to compare the photo to Karen. Then his mouth moved into something midway between a smirk and a snarl. "All right, Lieutenant, I see it. But I also see what the story is. This whole thing is a trap. The dean's call last night was a trick to make me think Gelman was getting the job. You wanted me to come after her so you could nab me."

Karen had had it. She grabbed his left arm and started to pull him out of the chair. But he swatted her hand away. "That's entrapment, you fool. Any case you think you have against me will get thrown out on its ass."

Now Karen was really done. She took a pair of handcuffs out of her pocket. "This is your last chance. Get up and put your hands behind your back."

Rather than complying, he held out his hands in front of him. "Here, you can put those on if you want to. The sooner we're done with this, the sooner I can call my lawyers."

I thought she was going to react forcefully, but she surprised me. After a moment, she shrugged and cuffed his hands in front of him. "Whatever. I don't want to waste any more time on you. Where are the kids?"

"You'll find them on the second floor, third door on the right. There's just one man watching them. See, Lieutenant, I'm always happy to cooperate with the law." He laughed again, this time with a touch of genuine amusement. "Just wait until my lawyers get their hands on this. I'll walk, and you'll be back to writing parking tickets."

This time it was Karen who put on the mocking smile. "Don't count on it. Entrapment isn't a viable defense if the defendant was already disposed to commit the crime."

"And you think you'll be able to convince a jury that I had a predisposition to criminal acts? A distinguished Harvard professor? Take a look at the wall on your right."

It was covered with photographs of Horrigan with a variety of scientific and political luminaries. Including the governor and both senators from Massachusetts, as well as the last three presidents of the United States.

"Those'll be my character witnesses," he continued. "And my lawyers will make O. J. Simpson's dream team look like junior high school debaters."

I had to admit, he sounded convincing. I wasn't acquainted with the laws governing entrapment, but there was no question that's what we'd done.

I glanced over at Carolyn and Martin to see their reactions to Horrigan's bluster. Martin's face was impassive. But Carolyn looked shaken. I could almost hear her thinking, *My God, he's going to get away with it!*

I waited for Karen's response, hoping it would be convincing enough to offer Carolyn some reassurance. But she ignored Horrigan and turned to Martin. "Do you mind watching this piece of shit while the rest of us go get the kids?"

"Sure. No problem."

Karen thanked him and started toward the door. I followed her, but Carolyn stayed where she was. And then she made a surprising request.

"I'm going to stay here with Martin. Karen, you and Brad can go. Just bring my children back safely."

"You don't have to do that," Karen said. "Come with us. Martin won't have any trouble handling this blowhard."

"Absolutely, go ahead Carolyn," Martin seconded. "I just hope he tries something and gives me the chance to beat the crap out of him."

But she stood firm. "No, I'll be more comfortable staying here. Just in case you need a hand."

CHAPTER 49

Still baffled by Carolyn's behavior, I followed Karen out of the office. She turned to me as we started up the staircase. "Do you understand what just went on? Staying behind is the last thing I expected Carolyn to do."

"No, it doesn't make any sense to me either. Seeing that her kids are safe has been at the top of her list since this started."

"You think she got cold feet at the last minute? Maybe she didn't want to go with us in case something went wrong," Karen suggested.

"That doesn't sound like Carolyn. But who knows. Let's get the kids back, and we can see what she says later. You need to talk to her about Horrigan's entrapment bullshit, too. I could tell it worried her. You don't think there's anything to it, do you?"

Karen frowned and sighed. "I wish I could say for sure. I'm comfortable that what we did was within bounds. But his lawyers will no doubt make the argument, and the fact is you can never be sure what's going to happen when a case goes to trial. Especially with the kind of lawyers he'll get, and people like former presidents as character witnesses."

That was far from reassuring. And it certainly wouldn't help

Carolyn. But we'd reached the top of the stairs, so rather than saying anything more, I pointed at the third door. "This one?"

"Yeah. Let's go in fast with our guns drawn. The guy inside shouldn't be expecting us, and with any luck we'll take him by surprise."

She was right. We burst into the room, and the shocked guard surrendered without a fight. Karen secured him to a chair, and we turned to the kids. They'd been sitting on a couch watching TV, but as soon as they saw us, Gail shrieked, "Aunt Karen!" and they came running over.

Karen put her arms around them both in a group hug. Even Bobby joined in, which I thought was notable for a twelve-year-old boy.

"Everything's fine now," Karen assured them. "Your mom's downstairs waiting for you. Are you both okay?"

"We're good." Bobby spoke with the authority of an older brother. The man in charge. "The dinner they gave us sucked, but everything else was all right."

I tousled his hair. "Good man. Let's go downstairs. I know your mom can't wait to see you."

Karen held Gail's hand as we went down to the first floor. Bobby and I followed behind them, walking side by side—no handholding for us men. We were moving quickly, anxious to reunite Carolyn with her children.

But then a shot rang out.

Karen yelled for the kids to stay where they were, and the two of us raced into the office. *Had Horrigan somehow managed to get a weapon? With both Martin and Carolyn on watch?*

I was prepared for a gunfight when we burst through the door. But I wasn't ready for what was in front of us.

Horrigan was lying on his back in the middle of the floor. With a bullet hole in his forehead and a growing puddle of blood under his head.

Karen ran over and knelt to exam the body. Her face was ashen when she looked up. "What happened? Are the two of you okay?"

Carolyn answered in a voice devoid of emotion. "We're fine. He was trying to escape, and I had to shoot him."

Karen furrowed her brow. "I don't understand. He was shot in the forehead. And it doesn't take a forensic expert to see it was from only a few inches away."

"He was trying to run," Carolyn said. "He'd gotten around Martin and was almost on top of me, ready to attack. There wasn't anything else I could do."

Martin jumped in to back her up, as if on cue. "I don't know how, but he knocked me over and was about to run Carolyn down. He was like a wild man, didn't her leave any choice." He glanced over at Horrigan's body. "She did what she had to do, and an evil man got what he deserved."

I didn't buy it. Martin was twenty pounds heavier and in much better shape. Horrigan couldn't have knocked him down, especially wearing handcuffs. And then we were supposed to believe he ran up to Carolyn so that her gun was almost against his forehead?

No, this was an execution. Not a foiled escape attempt.

Karen was looking at them with obvious disbelief when we heard someone knocking at the front door. Rather than addressing the matter further, she turned away from the body.

"Sounds like our backup is here. I'll need to tell them what's going on. Carolyn, your kids are waiting in the hall. Go ahead out to them while I talk to the detectives."

Carolyn hurried out of the office with Martin right behind her. They'd become attached quickly. A bond forged in combat, now strengthened by a shared conspiracy.

I didn't see how they could hope to get away with it. Not after Karen had examined the body. I could only imagine what she was going through. I wanted to tell her to let it go, to look the other way. But how could she? No doubt her heart was with Carolyn, as was mine. It was easy enough to understand what had happened. Carolyn had been afraid that Horrigan would get off, and horrified by what he'd planned for her kids, had taken the matter into her own hands.

Easy to understand, and at least for me, to forgive. But still murder in the eyes of the law. And Karen's entire adult life had been dedicated to law enforcement, ever since 2001 when she joined the police instead of going to law school as her response to the horrors of September 11.

She had to be in a state of unspeakable conflict, but in the end what choice did she have? As close to Carolyn as she was, I could only imagine her doing what the law required.

It would be hard for her. And for me. But I'd have to swallow my feelings for Carolyn and give Karen my full support.

I reached over and gave her shoulder a reassuring squeeze. "I'm sorry, I know how awful this has to be for you. Carolyn must have been so worried about Horrigan's lawyers succeeding with an entrapment defense that she lost it. Maybe she can even argue temporary insanity. Are you going to question her? It might be easier to have one of your detectives take it from here. Dick Lowe could handle it, couldn't he?"

She turned to me, and I was surprised to see a look of quiet determination in her eyes. I'd expected to find something else. Maybe dismay or sadness, but not calm resolve. She must have already come to peace with her commitment to uphold the law.

But what she said next astonished me.

She shook her head and smiled faintly. "There's no need for anyone to question her. She and Martin already told us what happened. Carolyn was forced to shoot the prisoner while he was trying to escape. He'd knocked Martin out of the way and was about to attack her; she couldn't do anything else. I'll give my report to Dick, and he can take it from there. While the four of us squeeze into the van with the kids and go home."

I was overwhelmed with relief, but at the same time I couldn't believe what I'd just heard. "But . . . you know they're not telling the truth," I stammered.

She must have sensed my complicated mixture of feelings and squeezed my hand to let me know she was at peace. "Martin was telling the truth when he said that an evil man got what he deserved. Would we accomplish something by destroying Carolyn's life?" She shook her head again. "No, the law was never meant to stand alone. Its purpose is to serve justice."

I looked over at Horrigan's body and nodded. "Justice has been served."

ACKNOWLEDGMENTS

I'm once again immensely grateful to my early readers, Alexandra Zilz and Shrabastee Chakraborty, for their thoughtful input. Their comments and suggestions continue to provide critical guidance and insight, without which Brad and Karen would risk going astray.

As always, it's a pleasure to thank Audrey Capuano for her continuing support, patience, and helpful thoughts. As well as for coining Karen's favorite line, "Of course I'm right. I'm always right."

And I'm delighted to thank Jennifer Caven (Mainly Words) for her outstanding editing and Evgeniia Gurcheva for a stunning cover design.

ABOUT THE AUTHOR

Geoffrey M. Cooper is an award-winning author of medical thrillers and a 2023 Maine Literary Award Finalist in Crime Fiction. His experience as a former cancer researcher and scientific administrator, having held positions at Harvard Medical School and Boston University as professor, department chair, and associate dean, now provides extensive background for his novels. He lives in Ogunquit, Maine.

Website: https://geofcooper.com/

Reviews from readers are greatly appreciated. If you enjoyed *The Plagiarism Plot*, please let other readers know by leaving your comments on Amazon or Goodreads.